Wolves of Endless Twilight

By Scott Perry

PublishAmerica
Baltimore

© 2007 by Scott Perry.
All rights reserved. No part of this book may be reproduced, stored in a retrieval system or transmitted in any form or by any means without the prior written permission of the publishers, except by a reviewer who may quote brief passages in a review to be printed in a newspaper, magazine or journal.

First printing

All characters in this book are fictitious, and any resemblance to real persons, living or dead, is coincidental.

At the specific preference of the author, PublishAmerica allowed this work to remain exactly as the author intended, verbatim, without editorial input.

ISBN: 1-4241-9072-X
PUBLISHED BY PUBLISHAMERICA, LLLP
www.publishamerica.com
Baltimore

Printed in the United States of America

For Tiffany
Thanks for believing in me

Wolves of Endless Twilight

To Steve
Enjoy
10-27-07

— Scott Perry

Chapter 1

Gavon Stills entered the smoke-filled tavern and took stock of the occupants in the dim lighting. This little dive differed little from any other in countless coastal towns and cities around the world and was complete with the usual cast of characters. But none of the others contained what he was seeking.

The newcomer rubbed his eyes to alleviate the stinging sensation brought on by the thick wall of cigarette smoke that slowly engulfed him. Three, of the dozen or so, stools at the bar were occupied by drunken old men discussing how the world had gone to Hell since they were young. Apparently the Democrats were to blame. Gavon simply shook his head and continued to scan the room. Finally his gaze settled on a scene at the far side of the tavern.

Across the room were two biker-looking types, apparently no longer interested in their game of pool. They were instead staring intently at a small group of people in the far corner of the room. Evidentially there was something of interest in the back of the bar. So, Gavon's eyes followed the gaze of the other onlookers.

He scanned past the under aged-girls who were looking at him and whispering to each other. In his younger wilder days this would have been a good thing. But he was older and wiser now, and not to mention taken.

At any rate he was past that sort of nonsense, so he continued to scan the room. Finally he saw what he had come to find.

In the far corner of the dimly lit tavern sat a man in his early thirties, with a pint of Guinness in one hand. He was apparently involved in a heated argument with a couple of locals in cowboy hats. Well, it was heated from the point of view of the two cowboys, who were clearly angry. But the man with the black beer seemed to be having a very good time with the situation and was actually smiling as he verbally sparred with the pair. He was leaning back in his chair with the same kind of look someone might have while watching a Monty Python movie.

The smiling man had curly black hair down to his shoulders. He was dressed in jeans and a black T-shirt that read Lombardi's Tavern, Hancock New York. His black leather jacket was casually draped over an unoccupied chair to his right. In spite of the fact that he was seated, it was apparent that he was slightly taller than the average male. His face was fair, but not pale, and apparently it hadn't been shaved in a few days. But his most striking feature was the look of his eyes, which were large, deep green, and wild. This feature gave him a slightly cat-like appearance.

Gavon overheard one of the cowboys half speak and half yell, while balling his fists, at the man in the corner. "My Grampa ain't no fuckin' monkey!"

To which the man with the pint replied with a laugh, "Well, I certainly can't tell by looking at his grandson. I mean seriously, the sloping forehead, beady little eyes. And I'm guessing you have some sort of stone tool in your pocket. Which is it, a blade flake or a hand axe?" He laughed again. But before either could say a word, the verbal onslaught continued. "My god, I thought that all of you were extinct. Are you Cro-Magnon or Neanderthal?" The man paused for a moment and took another drink.

The other stood still and glared back at him without saying a word.

When he didn't answer the drinking man sighed and continued. "I guess you don't know. Hey, I have a friend who is an anthropologist, maybe if you come with me we can get this sorted out. This find might just make me famous. Just as long as you aren't Homo erectus, I don't swing that way." And then he burst into a fresh fit of laughter. This seemed to push the two cowboys right over the edge and they moved in to educate him on the finer points of bar etiquette.

Gavon let out a sigh. He couldn't recall how many times had he gone to some little dive, that any respectable person wouldn't set foot in, to collect his friend only to find him involved in some sort of confrontation with a group of people who had been drinking too much liquid dumb-ass. Fortunately, the green eyed man knew how to handle himself and was probably not in any real danger. In fact the two men attacking him were far more likely to be injured than their intended victim.

Gavon's friend had grown up in Halifax, in the United Kingdom with his mother, who had been a bartender, as well as raising a son by herself. Consequently the earlier male influences in his life had been something a little short of the upper crust of society. When she had died shortly after his twelfth birthday, he had been forced to grow up in an overcrowded Catholic orphanage. This string of seemingly detrimental events had, in reality, prepared this man to deal with anything that life threw at him, although it had left him a little off center when it came to sanity. His ability to endure, and in this case deal out, hardship was something that the two drunken cowboys were about to witness first hand.

The first attacker threw a punch at the green-eyed man, but quickly realized that he had made a mistake. In one smooth, almost inhuman, motion the man in the corner slid from his chair. He then moved to the side to avoid the second fist that was aimed at his nose, and kicked the legs out from under his would-be attacker. Amazingly, he didn't spill a single drop of his beer. While taking a step back and letting the second man trip over the first, Gavon's friend turned his glass up and downed the rest of the dark liquid with such grace that it would have made a frat boy weep with pride. He then set the glass on a nearby table, burped loudly at his attackers, and smiled at the pair again.

The second man had stumbled at first, and apparently stepped on a sensitive part of the prone man, judging by the girlish squeal that came from the one on the floor. But finally he negotiated his way over his companion and attempted to swing at the smiling beer drinker. Gavon started to say something, but the green-eyed man saw the attack and dealt with it. In another fluid motion he took hold of the attacker's arm as it sped towards him, moved slightly to the side, and pulled. The cowboy realized he was off balance and tried to correct it. But when he stepped forward the other man simply moved in the opposite direction and deposited the unfortunate fellow on the floor. Well more or less on the floor, he landed on top of his friend, who was attempting to stand back up. There was an audible thump as the two fell back to the ground. Gavon's friend stood chuckling to himself and shaking his head, "Well, do you feel better now? I guess this is how you resolve disputes in your tribe. Most inhospitable, I'll be sure to speak to your chieftain or witch doctor when I see him."

The man on the top of the heap tried to get up, but Gavon's friend simply brought a boot down onto his hand as he tried to push himself into a position from which he could stand. The cowboy let out a yelp and pulled the injured hand back to protect it. This caused him to fall back on top of his companion, who once again had the wind knocked out of him.

The green-eyed man stood watching the two and laughing to himself for a moment. Then he picked up his glass. He turned it up one more time and then with a disappointed look on his face, set the empty container back on the table. Gavon's friend then turned to face the sound of one person slowly clapping. The victorious man began to bow as if he was a performer at the end of his act. But he quickly realized that the person clapping was his friend, who looked anything but amused. The man sighed again, took a hopeful glance at the bar and then spoke to the heap of arms and legs cursing at him from the floor. "Well, I guess my discovery will have to wait. It appears that I am needed elsewhere. It's been loads of fun."

With that the man quickly picked up his jacket and walked to the bartender, who was watching with a dumbfounded look on his face. He reached into his jacket and pulled out a twenty. "Sorry about the mess Jason," his voice gave away the hint of a British accent. Then he casually walked over to Gavon who looked at him, shook his head, and then followed him out the door.

The pair walked for about a minute in silence. Finally Gavon spoke, "Logan, why do you do this to me?"

Logan smiled, "What do you mean, you weren't even there. Well, not for the good parts anyway. You can't judge the whole performance on just the finale."

"You know what I mean. Every time you get into a confrontation with the locals…or the police," Gavon shot him a harsh glance, "Director Mitchell drags me into his office to see if I can talk some sense into you. And every time it seems like I fail."

Logan sighed, "Well, you always were the responsible one. Keep trying, maybe some day it will sink in."

"Somehow I doubt that. But I guess I can't give up on you just yet. Why do you continue to do this sort of thing anyway? I mean you are a respected member of society now, not some drunken soccer hooligan, at least not anymore."

Logan shrugged, "I guess I do it to try to stay sane."

Gavon laughed, "I think that you crossed that line a long time ago, probably before I met you."

"You question my sanity? That's pretty funny coming from someone who climbs cliffs for fun."

"We've been over this before. Rock climbing is a perfectly safe sport if you know what you are doing. People who get hurt are usually doing something stupid anyway. Besides Lynn's a climber as well, would you say that she's crazy?"

"No, she has a reason to climb around on rocks. She is a geologist after all. But you do it just for the hell of it. How is that sane?"

"How is what I do different from all of the other people participating in football, soccer, or any other sport anywhere in the world? I mean a lot of them carry some kind of risk of bodily harm. Would you rather I play golf or how about curling? Then there would be very little chance of me being seriously injured, unless I drop my beer on my toe or something."

"I think that you are a little young yet to take an interest in such things. Besides, you have to be really drunk and really bored to be any good at curling. Or maybe once you are playing such a stupid game you just don't care anymore. I mean it's the last step before you start wearing Bermuda shorts, black socks, and sandals while using a metal detector on the beach. But I digress. Would you explain something to me?"

"Sure."

"Sports have some sort of objective, correct?"

"I guess so." Gavon rolled his eyes. He was unsure where this was headed, but knew that he was going to have to let Logan finish or he'd never hear the end of it.

"Of course they do", Logan continued, "Otherwise there would be no point. I just don't understand participating in a sport where you are considered a winner if you don't die."

Gavon laughed, "I guess you have a point."

Logan always could make him feel good, even when he was the one who had been the original cause for annoyance. It had been that way since they had met, over ten years ago.

The Brit's antics had gotten the two of them into trouble on many occasions, most of the time after a good night of drinking. Part of the problem stemmed from the fact that the green-eyed man's accent, which sounded like a mix of English and Scottish, got thicker with every beer.

Combine that with slurred words and Logan became almost impossible to understand when he was drunk. As a result of this, Gavon had been his friend's translator to the police in seven states and counting. But this was not something that he listed on his resume. Although drunken British translator was certainly a valuable skill to have.

It wasn't that Logan was a bad person, in fact he was about the best friend anyone could have. He just was willing to step over the line of legality, and accepted social norms in order to have a laugh. One good example of this was an incident that had occurred one summer when the two were undergrads. The pair had managed to land jobs at a summer camp in upstate New York. Interestingly this was the spark that had inspired them both to go into teaching.

One night after the local tavern had shut down for the night and, as a result, kicked them out, Logan convinced his friend to go to the drive-through of a local fast food restaurant, despite the fact it was obviously closed. The two had pulled up in Gavon's truck to find the lights mostly turned off and a lone worker inside, mopping the floor. When the man simply looked at them and continued cleaning the floor Logan crawled across Gavon, who was driving, and knocked on the window of the drive-through.

The worker came to the window and told the drunken Englishman that the store was closed. Not to be deterred Logan climbed through the now open window, past the terrified minimum wage earner, and began mopping while telling the stunned man that if he would cook up some food for them, he would finish the floor.

All of this may have been rather humorous to the fast food employee, except for the fact that Logan had been drinking all night and was unintelligible to everyone but Gavon, who was still in the car shaking his head and cursing under his breath. Needless to say the police were called and Logan was taken to jail. Fortunately Gavon was able to convince the restaurant not to press charges. In fact, even the police had a good laugh once the whole story was explained to them by the Brit's translator. One of them even joked that the restaurant should pay Logan for his work. The duo had even made it back to camp in time for breakfast.

Gavon laughed to himself. They had certainly had some interesting times together. Fortunately for him those days were in his past and he was slowly getting Logan to follow him on the road to responsibility, although his friend was still clearly lagging behind.

"So I guess the ship's ready to sail?" Logan's question snapped Gavon back into the present.

"Yep, the only thing we were missing was a pain in the ass biochemist. Fortunately I just found one."

Logan laughed, "Should I renew my complaint about the lack of proper adult beverages on this little adventure?"

Gavon laughed, his friend would probably never change. "I would wait until Mitchell calms down a bit, he is not terribly happy with you right now. Besides, it wasn't his choice. Our sponsor is providing us with the ship, without which we couldn't get to our destination. You know what Alaskan waters are like in the winter, especially where we are going. So when you can come up with an ice-breaker, then you can make the rules."

"Six months without a beer. How could anyone be expected to think clearly? Don't they know that people could die because of that decision? I mean why don't they just ban coffee too and then give us all weapons while they are at it."

Gavon laughed again. "Lynn and I managed to smuggle a few bottles of liquor on board, but that won't last for the whole trip. But we may be able to restock when we dock in Anchorage for the rest of our supplies. If you'd tried, you could have gotten at least something onboard."

"What makes you think that I didn't?" the Englishman said slyly.

"What?" Gavon turned to his friend, not liking where this conversation was probably going to lead.

"Did they load all of the equipment from my lab like they were supposed to?" Logan smirked.

"I think so. Why?" Gavon knew he wasn't going to like the answer, but he asked anyway.

Logan smirked a little more. "Those cans about the size of a can of beans are actually concentrated malted barley extract and the little bags of rabbit food are really pellets of hops. Shall I tell you where I hid the yeast?"

"You're going to brew beer in the lab!?" Gavon acted amazed, but he had half expected his friend to try something like this. And in reality was happy that his brew-master friend was going to provide refreshment on the voyage. But he had to feign disapproval, at least a little.

"Of course not, that would be an open invitation for Mitchell or one of the churchies to find, and sabotage my efforts to bring a little joy into the world. They were nice enough to give us all our own rooms, the perfect hiding place for an ordinary batch of grain to turn into something truly fit for human consumption. Which reminds me, are they really making you and Lynn sleep separately?"

"They think they are. But what are they going to do once we are underway? I'm not going to put up with their outdated notions of morality, even if they are paying for my research. Once we are out to sea, I'm moving into Lynn's room. I got a couple of undergrads to put my things in there while we're loading. I assume you are going to help me if they try to throw me overboard?"

Logan laughed again. "That depends, when is your sister coming back to visit? I may consider helping you if you put in a good word for me."

"Logan, you may be my best friend, but if you ever touch my sister I will have to cut off your twig and giggle berries."

"Oh well, I had to try."

The two shared a laugh and made their way to the ship.

When they got there they saw a small man standing on the dock, apparently waiting for something. Once he saw them the shorter man began to rapidly walk down the stairs from the ship towards the pair with a facial expression that could only mean one of two things. He was either very angry or he was constipated. Neither Gavon nor Logan thought it was the latter.

It was all Gavon could do not to burst into a fit of laughter when Logan muttered, "Beware, the malignant dwarf approaches."

Chapter 2

Linus Mitchell was a short man. Short meaning just over five feet tall. His diminutive size was emphasized whenever he was around Logan and Gavon, both of whom were right around six. In an equally cruel twist of fate nature had seen fit to equip him with squinty eyes and a rather long and pointed nose, giving him a somewhat rat-like appearance. On top of his appearance, a childhood of dealing with bullies had given him the temperament of a Chihuahua.

He tried to make up for his shortcomings, no pun intended, by lashing out at everyone around him, making him virtually friendless. People like Logan Fry, good looking, intelligent, and successful seemed to infuriate him more than anything else. Everything always seemed to work out for Doctor Fry, even when he didn't put forth much effort. Linus, on the other hand had to work harder than he thought possible in order to compete with those people who had natural ability.

As the two approached him, he knew that Logan had made some sort of smart assed comment, based on the look on Gavon's face. Of the two Gavon Stills had always been the lesser headache. Both were amazingly talented scientists, but sometimes they acted in a less than dignified manner in Mitchell's eyes. After all rock music and beer had no place in the refined circles of the university professor.

Linus had risen from his position as professor of Entomology to Director of Life Sciences at West Tangiers University a few years before Gavon and Logan were hired as the new Mammalogy and Biochemistry professors, respectively. So Linus was their boss, at least in theory. But the truth of it was the dean of the College of Sciences, Lola Kimmel, had hired the two young professors directly, bypassing Mitchell all together. What made matters worse, at least in the eyes of the director, was the fact that both had been grad-students of Kimmel when she had been a professor at UCLA and she thought very highly of them both. Gavon was even listed as a co-author in several of Kimmel's more well-known books.

Having such talented scientists on staff was certain to add to the university's prestige. After all West Tangiers was a relatively new university and needed to make a name for its self. It had been founded two years before Linus had been hired. And when the first man to hold his position had been killed in a car accident, Mitchell was promoted to fill the gap. He had held the post ever since. But everyone on staff knew that the only reason for his promotion to director was because Lynn Levandusky had declined the position since it would take time away from her research. And Lynn saw herself as a scientist, not a bureaucrat.

Such a situation put Linus in a difficult position. He wanted to be rid of Logan more than anything else in his career, perhaps even in his life. But his only issue was the man's personality. The crazy Brit had managed to find his way out of every situation that could potentially result in his termination, partially because of his ties to Kimmel, but mostly because of his abilities. This created a problem for Mitchell. Logan was virtually untouchable, and knew it. He simply had to put up with his antics, no matter how irritating they were.

Ironically Logan's quirkiness, while infuriating to Mitchell, had made him one of the most beloved professors among the students, and not just among the science majors. There were even students majoring in English and other unrelated subjects who used their elective credits to take classes taught by "Crazy Doctor Fry," who once gave an hour long lecture in his bathrobe and a paper hat that said "Happy New Year." So there was really nothing he could do to rid himself of the man who was constantly causing trouble for him.

Gavon was the less troublesome of the two, although he was relatively certain that it had been this man who had released about 50 crickets into his office a few months ago. The large number of spiders Linus kept there had prevented him from being able to call an exterminator. So all he could do was be patient until the insects finally starved. The chirping had nearly driven him to madness, before the last one finally died and was silent.

Still, Gavon was more soft spoken and reserved than Logan, but no less talented as a scientist and teacher. He had met Logan Fry in his sophomore year at Cornell. After that fateful encounter the two had become good friends. Now the duo was making Mitchell's already stressful life even more so.

As a result of his more palatable personality and close ties to Logan, not to mention Mitchell's poor people skills, Gavon often served as the go between for the Brit and the director. Things were simply easier that way. That had been the case on this day as well. Mitchell had sent Professor Stills to find the rogue biochemist and bring him back so the ship could leave on time. He was slightly pleased to see that Doctor Stills had accomplished his mission. But the mere sight of Doctor Fry immediately sent his mood south.

Once the two professors were standing in front of him, Linus opened his mouth, but then stepped back onto the stairs leading into the ship in order to be on a more even level to the two taller men. Finally he began to speak.

"Where have you been Mr. Fry?"

"I believe that's Doctor Fry, Linus," Logan responded in a casual sort of way, while he inspected the finger nails on his left hand.

"Fine, Dr. Fry where have you been?" Linus seemed to be getting more and more agitated by the second.

"I was finishing up a last-minute experiment. It ran longer than I thought it would," Logan replied as he cast a sideways glance at his friend, who just shook his head and mouthed the word "don't". Gavon knew that one of Logan's goals in life was to make Linus Mitchell's head explode.

"Somehow I doubt that, especially since all of your equipment is onboard the ship already," Director Mitchell snapped back. And even before Logan spoke Gavon rolled his eyes, knowing full well that his friend was going to see how far he could push the smaller man before he made him crack. His goal in every encounter seemed to be to make Mitchell as angry as possible, and he was good at it.

"No really, it was a behavioral experiment. I was seeing how stress and certain chemicals evoke aggressive reactions in some primates."

"Okay, I'll play along. How did this experiment turn out?" Linus sighed.

"Pretty much how I figured it would," Logan said with a grin.

Linus knew from experience that this conversation was going nowhere so he let it drop before he gave Logan the satisfaction of seeing him lose his temper. As he turned to ascend the gangway into the ship he noticed a silver haired man dressed completely in black with the exception of the small square of white in the middle of his collar coming down the stairs to meet them. He was followed by a man who was dressed as a sailor and, judging by the ridiculous tri-cone hat he was wearing, could only be the ship's captain. The mariner looked the part as he walked casually down the stairs behind the clergyman. He did seem more than a little overweight for a sailor, but the grizzled look of his face told all that the extra weight was not a permanent feature. The mariner had a rough, sea hardened look about him and deep piercing eyes, which scanned the group coldly, before he nodded, put a cigarette to his lips, and struck a match.

The cleric looked somewhat friendlier, but there was still something about him that made Gavon uneasy, although he wasn't quite sure what it was. After a moment he decided that it was probably just the fact that the other man was clergy, and Gavon was a man of science. But he still couldn't shake the feeling that the friendly smile was there to hide something darker.

As Logan was opening his mouth, Mitchell turned and shot a venomous gaze at him and growled, "No alter boy comments!"

Logan closed his mouth, snickered a little, began to open it again then seemed to think better of it and simply shrugged.

The bishop descended the gangway until he was within a few feet of the group. Linus shot another harsh glance at Logan and then turned to greet the newcomer with a smile. "Hello Father Devaney."

Father Marco Devaney smiled warmly at the group. "Ah, you must be Doctor Logan Fry. It is a pleasure to make your acquaintance."

Logan simply nodded and said, "Hi". Then he began to study the San Francisco bay rather intently. Maybe it contained a way to get away from this priest. He still remembered his days in the care of such men and was not capable of trusting them in the slightest. His personal problems with the Catholic Church were compounded by those he shared with Gavon and most other scientists.

The presence of clergy, who openly rejected some of the most important parts of the biological sciences, on a legitimate scientific expedition did not sit well with any of them. As a result they looked on these priests with suspicion and contempt. And rightly so, the church had long been an enemy of the sciences. But since this bishop's order was footing the bill as well as supplying the ship, Gavon and Logan had let the matter drop with Mitchell and had agreed to at least make an attempt at civility in their presence.

This was potentially a ground breaking expedition. A couple of years before, an expedition into the Alaskan wilderness had reported seeing

Grizzly bears wandering around at night to the north of Nome, Alaska. Normally this would not be any big deal, but this was the total night of the arctic winter. The bears should have been well into the deep slumber of hibernation. Such behavior had never been seen, much less documented. So this discovery had the potential to catapult West Tangiers into the spotlight in the world of the biological sciences. There were also reports of other animals staying active when they should be dormant. So, despite their personal reservations and suspicions, Gavon and Logan understood that this could be a major discovery, and tried to keep quiet.

Linus on the other hand thought that the church's new campaign of embracing the sciences was an excellent idea. He after all was something of an enigma. As the director of Life Sciences and an accomplished biologist in his own right. Director Mitchell was, at the very least, influential in scientific circles. But he was also a devout Catholic. Gavon and Logan always had wondered how such a thing was possible since a large portion of Christians did not even believe in Evolution. Some of these people were still trying to get the ridiculous notion of "intelligent design" taught in classrooms alongside legitimate scientific theories. Never the less Linus was both very pious and a scientist, without seeing any kind of conflict.

The funding of this and possibly other expeditions by the church was part of a larger public relations campaign launched by the new pope to portray the Catholic Church as a modern organization with something to offer the people of the new millennia. This campaign had programs all over the world, but its focus was primarily the United States, where Catholicism had been on the decline for a number of years.

The priest sex scandals and other kinds of controversy had caused many Catholics to simply walk away and non-Christians to become more and more mainstream. The church had begun other programs, on a smaller scale, in many European countries as well. Gavon and Logan had joked that the reason for the church focusing on the most advanced countries was the clear fact that education seemed to be the best vaccine for religion. This seemed to scare the church more than a little bit. But, there was really no sense in denying the obvious fact that as intelligence increased, piety often decreased.

The idea of sending clergy on the expeditions was in order encourage dialogue between the scientific community and the church. By putting people on an extended voyage with priests, the two groups would eventually begin to talk to one another and hopefully begin to set aside their differences. They might even begin to try to work together.

This was of course what was said in public, but the scientists were pretty sure that it was just another thinly veiled attempt to convert them and as a result keep them from speaking out against the church at every turn. They didn't know just how right they would be.

As soon as it seemed appropriate Gavon mentioned that he needed to check on some things in the cargo hold, and moved past Devaney and the captain. He then proceeded up the steps onto the upper deck of the large vessel, with Logan following closely at his heals.

Chapter 3

The captain, Devaney, and Mitchell remained outside to discuss some of the logistics of the voyage and to supervise the dock workers, who were loading the final crates of equipment into one of the ship's two main holds. Gavon and Logan continued to walk up the stairs into the ship.

The Perseverance was a nuclear powered ice breaker that had been purchased for a bargain when the Soviet Union had collapsed. It had a heavily reinforced hull for negotiating the ice filled waters of the northern seas and had served in many kinds of roles throughout its many years in service. On many occasions saving fishermen who had become trapped in pack ice and patrolling the Soviet ports to keep the shipping lanes open.

At over 300 feet in length, it was more than capable of transporting all of the equipment necessary for the expedition as well as having several of the smaller rooms that had once served as crew quarters converted into temporary labs for the scientists to perform experiments as needed. The interior had been upgraded to be rather comfortable, for a ship. And the quarters for the professors resembled those that a person would find on a cruise ship, not a Soviet era ice breaker.

The size of the ship also enabled it to carry enough supplies to support the scientists and crew if it became trapped in the ice and needed to wait until spring in order to leave. Such a thing was a very real possibility even for a ship designed to break through the ice, and had been planned for.

There was even a crane on the aft section of the ship that could lift heavy equipment from a large door in the deck that opened to the large cargo bay. This crane was large enough to swing equipment well away from the ship and onto stable ice. Trying to lower heavy equipment like a snow cat onto ice that had just been broken up by the ship's movements would be a very expensive mistake.

The labs were located on the second deck and the quarters for the crew and scientists were located on the lower deck. The cargo holds took up large portions the ship at the stern. Each one was roughly forty feet long and forty feet wide. Twenty feet up was the ceiling which contained a large door, so the crane could be used to move the equipment. There was also a smaller door to allow people to enter and exit at the floor level.

One of these was to be used for the equipment that would be necessary to track down the bears and other animals in the arctic winter. Snowmobiles, tranquilizer guns, and all manner of survival equipment were all packed safely in crates for the voyage. The second hold was to be used as a holding area for any of the larger animals that were to be captured, examined, tagged, and released.

All scientists were given their own rooms and Gavon's suggestion that he share a room with Lynn had been flatly denied. He viewed it as more archaic bullshit, but really didn't say much else on the matter. The pair had been together for over two years, living together for the latter half of that time. Professor Stills was not about to go on a six month voyage without sleeping in the same bed as the woman he loved, no matter who objected. He had a hard enough time sleeping as it was. The truth was, without her his nightmares would be even worse than the usually were.

All graduate students were forced to stay in the dorms with undergrads of the same sex. This was yet another attempt by the sponsors to keep fraternization to a minimum. Their plan failed for a number of reasons.

Among them was the fact that two of the male grad students were much more interested in each other than the girls in the other dorm. Another failure in the plan occurred when the responsibility for enforcement fell on the professors in charge of the trip, namely Lynn, Gavon, and Logan, whose views on the matter were hardly a secret. So they had delegated the responsibility of keeping tabs on the various couples to the grad students, nudge, nudge, wink, wink.

Gavon, in a thinly disguised act of defiance, had even let his grad students know that his room would be unoccupied in case any of the other couples wanted to use it. Meanwhile, his luggage had been moved to Lynn's room by the undergrads who had managed to get a seat on the ship. He and Lynn were not going to announce this decision, but they also weren't going to go out of their way to hide it either.

The students, grad and undergrad alike, on the expedition were housed in two large rooms with bunk beds. The men were on one side of the ship and the women were on the other with the rooms housing the professors, and Director Mitchell in between. These dorms were not nearly as lavishly furnished as those of the professors and there was a community bathroom with several shower stalls attached to each. The crew members were housed on the deck above them in a similar manner. But the priests and the captain were given their own rooms.

Gavon and Logan looked at each other. Mitchell and Devaney had not said anything to either of them. So it looked like everything had gone according to plan. Once they were out of earshot of the director and the bishop, Gavon turned to his friend.

"So, how long until you can have a batch of beer ready?"

Logan smiled, "I told you it was a good idea."

"Okay, you're right. How long?"

"Give me a couple of days."

"You mean weeks don't you?"

"No, I developed a strain of yeast that works very quickly. I call it

Logan's Lightning. I've finally found a way to use my biochemistry training to benefit mankind. We will be in beer heaven before long. By the way how many bottles of booze did you manage to smuggle aboard?"

"Well, Lynn has four, two rum, one Jack, and one Bailey's. I think Lance and Steve have some as well."

"So the rump-wranglers in on this are they? Does anyone else have anything?"

"Hey, there is no need for that."

"I'm sorry, pillow biters."

"You're hopeless."

"Now don't get me wrong, I really like those two, just not in the same manner they like each other. Besides we have an understanding, they can call me Professor Limey and make references to the apparent lack of good orthodontists in my homeland, and I can call them rump wranglers, sometimes even butt pirates. But we all know that it is in good fun and we take it in stride."

"You really like to dance across that line of political correctness don't you?"

"Political correctness has never solved anything. In fact I think that if people would just learn to laugh a little more at the obvious humor of certain stereotypes we would all get along better."

"I do agree with you, but unfortunately most other people don't. So you should try to tone it down a little bit, if that is at all possible."

"I know who can take it and who can't. I never pick on someone who will take it the wrong way."

"Like Director Mitchell?"

"That is a special case. The man is such an insufferable dick that I enjoy making his life difficult."

"That mentality is going to get you fired."

Logan paused for a moment then looked at his friend. "You and I both know he can't fire either of us. Besides, I don't care if he likes me or not.

And at any rate it is rather fun having a nemesis. It makes me feel kind of like a super hero. Of course Linus is certainly not of the same quality as most super villains, but he's all I have to work with."

Gavon laughed, "Okay my crazy friend, here's my stop."

"Give her a big kiss for me."

"Brew your beer ass hole."

"Alright see you at tea…er dinner."

"Later."

Chapter 4

Gavon Stills chuckled to himself as he walked down the narrow metal tube that passed for a corridor. Being friends with Logan was never anything short of entertaining. How was it possible to bundle so much greatness and so much insanity into one person?

He sighed as he came to a nondescript looking door. It looked like every other door on the ship, made of steel with a wheel in the middle of it instead of a doorknob, but he would have known who was waiting inside the room without even looking at the numbers.

Gavon shared a bond with the woman in this room. It was something that he couldn't explain. Dr. Stills didn't believe in the supernatural at all. The idea of ESP made about as much sense as werewolves and the Easter Bunny. But for some reason he always knew when Lynn was close by. The scientist in him attributed it to something like a subtle smell or a certain distinct sound she made when she breathed. It must be something that he picked up on a subconscious level.

But the romantic in him insisted that it was something that defied explanation. Maybe there was something to the whole idea of soul mates. He laughed one more time, shook his head and turned the handle. Upon entering he found who he was looking for.

Lynn Levandusky had come into his life three years ago when he had been hired to teach Mammalogy. They had met when Gavon had simply walked into her office, introduced himself, and asked where a good place to get some lunch was near campus. He hadn't even seen her until that moment, but as soon as he laid eyes on her he knew he wanted to get to know her better. At the time he had no idea that she had been thinking the same thing.

Lynn had looked up from her desk, glanced at the clock and asked if he wanted some company. He had smiled and nodded and the two had enjoyed a delightful lunch at the local sushi restaurant. Both had been so caught up in conversation that they had been late to teach their 3:00 classes. They had arrived at the restaurant just after 11:30. That night they had gone out for drinks and talked the night away as if they had known each other since childhood. From there their relationship had blossomed from colleagues, to friends, and finally lovers.

Professor Stills stood in the doorway gazing at Lynn. One of her bags was on the bed and she had a shirt in one hand. It fell softly to the floor, completely missing the open dresser as she moved to the door to embrace him.

As he held her in his arms, she asked, "Where have you been troublemaker?"

He laughed and simply said, "Logan."

"Well, is everything okay?" she smiled.

"As well as could be expected I guess, other than a couple of pissed off rednecks, there was no harm done."

Lynn raised her eyebrows, "How did Logan find a red neck bar in San Francisco?"

"I don't know how he gets into the situations I find him in." He let out a small chuckle, "I've started just accepting it. But as usual it was a rather interesting thing to witness."

Gavon went on to tell her about the scene he had walked in on and Logan's plans to brew beer on the voyage. She laughed and then kissed him. She was truly beautiful. He stared into her blue eyes and stroked her long blond hair. He still couldn't believe that a woman like her wanted to be mixed up with a guy like him. But she did. Gavon was just thankful that he hadn't met her in college, when he was too wild and immature to really appreciate the wonderful person she was.

He was deeply in love with this woman. But her beauty was only an extra benefit, for Lynn was a truly brilliant person. She was a professor of Paleontology and Geology and was one of the few people Linus actually got along with. In truth there was not a single person that he had ever encountered who didn't get along with her. On top of that she was one of the most competent people he had ever met. No matter what the situation, he'd never known her to lose her composure. This was something he truly valued, as he had little patience for the stereotypical helpless female type.

Gavon had always suspected Linus was interested in her. Not in a colleague sort of way, but something along the lines of what he now shared with her. As a result the director had been more than a little irritated by the relationship Gavon had developed with Lynn. But he appeared to be over it at this point. So Doctor Stills didn't push the issue. There was no reason for him to feel threatened by someone like Linus Mitchell.

They held each other for a while, and then she got a look in her eyes that said, "You have entirely too many clothes on." He kissed her again and brushed her cheek with his hand, but before they could get any farther there was a knock on the door.

Gavon sighed and said, "Hold that thought."

He opened the door to see two people carrying his bags. He recognized them as two of the undergrads. Both looked somewhat nervous. Doctor Stills laughed at their expressions a little bit. To him they reminded him of his high school days when he'd come in late at night after a good night of drinking only to find his father waiting for him in the living room. After a moment the young woman, who was in front spoke up.

"Director Mitchell told us to take your bags to a room down the hall, but then Professor Fry said that Mitchell didn't know what he was talking about and said to bring them here. We aren't going to get in trouble are we?"

"Logan said that? Or was that the toned down version?"

The young woman simply blushed and looked at the metal floor of the hallway. Finally the young man behind her spoke up. "If you want a direct quote, he said that Linus Mitchell doesn't know his own ass from a crater on Mars, much less where my friend wants his luggage."

The man young man then broke into a grin, while the young woman looked more horrified. Then she looked at the professor as if to ask her question again.

Gavon laughed, "No you aren't going to be in trouble. I might, but not you two. Just set them on the bed and I'll take care of them."

Jaime was a senior biology major and was so timid she would make a frightened rabbit seem brave. Her shoulder length brown hair was pulled into a pony tail and her thick black rimmed glasses seemed appropriate considering her mousey personality and 4.0 GPA. But Gavon suspected that some of the male students realized that under the bookworm exterior was a very beautiful person, not so very different from the woman he was in love with. Although she had a panicky streak in her that was completely absent in his lover. Gavon and Lynn had each had her in a couple of classes and thought she would go far as a researcher and if she came out of her shell a little bit, she would be able to do anything she wanted to.

The man with her was named Ryan. He was a junior and reminded Gavon of a younger version of himself, in his pre-Logan days. He was the kind of person who wanted to keep his head down and not make any waves. Yet he had a practical joker side to him that was rarely seen. This was mostly due to the fact that Ryan took joy in the reaction of people to a well executed joke, not from receiving credit for it. He was even a fellow

Texan. Ryan's GPA was not as impressive as that of Jaime, but Gavon's hadn't been exceptional when he was 21 years old either.

The two set his bags down and began to leave. Then Ryan turned to Gavon and said, "I think Lance and Steve are looking for you Dr. Stills."

"Thanks Ryan, and since we are not in the classroom, you can call me Gavon, you too Jaime."

Jaime blushed, "We'll see you later Dr. Stills, Dr. Levandusky."

With that the two quickly exited the room and closed the door. Gavon turned back to Lynn, "Good kids," he said.

"I think Jaime has a bit of a crush on you honey."

"Yeah, probably, but she'll get over it, all the other students have."

"Well, at least you're modest about it," Lynn smiled.

Gavon brushed her cheek with his hand again and said, "Well, I guess I'd better find out what Lance and Steve want. Otherwise more people might start pounding on the door. Are you coming?"

She smiled and said, "Well I guess I'd better, you seem to be a popular man today."

"You don't need to worry. It's not like you have any competition, especially not from Lance and Steve. I don't swing that way."

"I don't know. I seem to recall a time when you kissed Logan, full on the lips at that. I can't even say for certain that there was no tongue." Lynn then shot a playful glance at him.

"That was different. Besides, the money I won on that little wager is paying for our vacation this summer. But it did worry me a little that he didn't really try to fight back."

Lynn laughed again and moved across the room to embrace him tightly. Then she looked at him and said, "I guess we'd better go. Otherwise they'll come looking for us. Maybe we'll get some alone time later."

The pair left their bags for later and proceeded down the hall. After a quick kiss, the two young professors went up on deck where they found

Logan, Lance, Steve, and another man who was wearing a beat up looking cowboy hat who had what appeared to be a rifle case slung over his shoulder.

Chapter 5

Gavon and Lynn smiled as they walked up to the quartet. As they approached Logan nodded to them and the others turned to look in their direction.

The man in the hat was the first to speak, his thick accent left no doubt that he was from Australia. "Well, well, look at this, Lynn and Gavon coming to say G'day to me, the Brit, and the pooftas."

At this last comment Lance and Steve rolled their eyes and shook their heads almost in unison. It was almost comical the way the two moved together. Lance turned to the Aussie and laughed, "Well at least I stick to my own species, how are the sheep these days Malcolm or have you moved on to Kangaroos yet?"

The Aussie laughed, "'Roo's are a bit too hard to catch and the sheep are getting a bit timid, we have had to look to goats and even cattle lately. They're a bit nastier, but the horns make it easier to hold on at least."

This time the whole group laughed. Malcolm had led several of the most recent expeditions for the university, and as a result had become pretty close with the grad students and the professors. Even Linus liked him, at least as much as Linus could like anyone, in spite of his crude behavior and sense of humor.

Malcolm then turned to look directly at Gavon and Lynn. "So, I guess you two are still an item."

Gavon smiled again, "Yes we are." He then put his hand around his lover.

"But I don't see any rings yet, so I guess there is still hope for me."

Lynn laughed, "Malcolm, you are too much like a brother to me for anything to ever happen."

Malcolm looked at her and tried to feign surprise. "No, not you sis, I was referring to Gavon. I mean, I'm sure that Lance and Steve have noticed. Your man has quite a nice ass!" Malcolm then proceeded to pretend to caress Gavon's chest while licking his lips seductively.

The whole group laughed again as Gavon pushed the Aussie away and rolled his eyes. His face made it pretty apparent that he was thinking something like, "Great, now I have to baby sit two of them."

Finally Lance composed himself enough to speak. He was a well built man in his mid twenties with blue eyes and raven black hair. "So, are the witch hunters going to be hounding us the entire time we are on this trip? Or are the only going to bother us if they think we might be enjoying ourselves?"

"I'm afraid that either way it will be a pain in the ass," Doctor Stills answered.

The blond man finally spoke up, "I heard that they aren't even letting you and Lynn share a room. Is that true?"

"They think it is Steve", Gavon replied. "Fortunately all of us are smart enough to figure out ways around their archaic rules. Which reminds me, you guys and the other students are going to have to work out some kind of system if you are going to be using the empty room. We don't want anyone barging in on something. When I was in college we hung a hook from a coat hanger on the door, it was a bit more subtle than a pair of panties or a bra."

"Yes, smart enough to keep your voices down as well." The voice had a thick Georgia accent and came from behind Gavon.

Professor Stills turned quickly to see the newcomer. Before him stood a man with a thick mustache and goatee, wearing a black cowboy hat, and a dusty black trench coat. To Gavon he looked very much like one of the stereotypical cowboys from the silly old movies he had been addicted to as a child. The Colt .45 on his hip and rifle over his shoulder only enhanced this image.

The man spoke up again. "Since you are so smart, I suppose you were already aware that you were talking loud enough for me to hear every word you said once I was within 30 feet. I would use the more nondescript metal hangers if I were you. The big white plastic ones really stand out against the grey of the doors."

Malcolm spoke up as he slapped the new man on the back. "Everyone, this is Quint, we were in the Legion together, and I can assure you that he is the best. Between the two of us, you people should be well protected from any of the more unpleasant things we might encounter on this little adventure. So all you need to worry about is doing all of the things that you grown up nerds like to do." Quint smiled almost invisibly beneath his thick mustache and goatee.

The newcomer then turned to Gavon, "Oh, I didn't mean anything by it, I'm pretty sure none of our bible toting chaperones heard anything of interest. And I sure as hell don't care for their rules either." As if to illustrate this point, Quint looked casually over his shoulder. Then when he was sure the coast was clear, he pulled a flask from inside his coat and took a sip. Then he offered it to Gavon, who smiled and accepted. After a small sip of the strong liquid that tasted like a mix of paint thinner and rocket fuel, the professor let out a small cough and handed the concoction back to the newcomer.

Quint nodded to indicate that things were fine between the two of them. Then spoke. "I apologize. Where are my manners? My mother would be furious. I have not introduced myself properly. I am Quintus Vale, gentleman adventurer, and I will be your guide on this little endeavor, along with Malcolm of course." Then he bowed to the group, who then proceeded to introduce themselves.

"Quint and I have had some interesting times to say the least, and he has even saved my life a couple of times in some god forsaken desert in Africa. But in spite of those lapses in judgment, I still think he's the best."

Malcolm wasn't exaggerating when he told the group of Quintus' skills. Apparently the man had been more highly trained than most others in the Foreign Legion and had been taught to use just about every weapon imaginable. After a couple of tours, he'd gone to work in the private sector doing the same sort of work as Malcolm. The Georgian had a very quiet way about him, but Gavon could tell by looking at this man's eyes that he was someone who had seen much, much more than anyone his age should have.

There was no doubt in anyone's mind that getting to know Quintus Vale would be a very unforgettable experience. But at least he was personable and apparently leaned a little closer to something that resembled sanity than his Australian counterpart or Logan.

After the introductions were over, the group decided to get a bite to eat in the ship's cafeteria before the vessel left port. This would give them a chance to get better acquainted with the newcomer. Besides, if they went early, maybe they could avoid Mitchell, Devaney, or the other two church officials.

Chapter 6

On September twenty-first, after dinner Gavon and Lynn sat on the deck of the ship watching the port of San Francisco fade into the night. This would be one of the last warm evenings that they would experience for a while. So they decided to take in the night air before it became so cold that this sort of thing would require arctic gear and goggles.

The voyage to the northern shores of Alaska would take a couple of months, not because of the distance, but because of the weather and ice they would encounter later on would make traveling in the ocean painfully slow. At first it would be a rather pleasant voyage, but later on it would get pretty rough as the seas would be filled with frozen islands and the days would get progressively shorter as the ship proceeded north into the arctic winter. And by the time they reached their destination, there would be no daylight at all.

The plan was to get to the destination by early December at the latest. The professors onboard were to teach one class each, which would consist of 8 undergrads. The six graduate students were to help the two excursion leaders, Malcolm and Quintus, with preparation for the research ahead, as well as assist the professors with the classes. Once they reached the research location, classes would be more sporadic and the students would begin learning in a more hands on kind of way.

As for the ever present religious contingent, they kept to themselves for the most part in the beginning. In fact, they seemed to spend an inordinate amount of time in Devaney's room with the door closed. This of course caused Logan to begin referring to the bishop's room as "The Closet." Most of the professors and students were rather pleased at the church's hands off approach. They were fine with being left alone.

The only one who even seemed to want to talk to any of the clerics was Linus. He and Father Devaney ate lunch together as if they were old friends. The two discussed the expedition and the mission of the order. Their plans were to minister an Inuit village near the research area. Devaney told the director that he and the two monks had been putting a lot of time into planning and studying the customs of the Inuit people.

"Yes, we plan to bring the word of God to those living in the most inhospitable place on Earth. Regrettably I won't be able to join them though." Devaney told Linus as he put a couple of sprinkles of salt into his stew.

"Why not?" Mitchell looked confused.

"I have some business in Anchorage that needs attention. Brother Jonathan and Brother Samuel are quite capable I assure you. Besides there will be other opportunities to see the North Country."

"I have no doubt of that. But isn't it a little disappointing for you? I mean you are going to be so close, only to miss out."

Devaney just smiled. To Gavon or Logan it would have seemed like something wicked. But Linus thought that it looked sincere and nodded.

Devaney looked up to see Doctor Stills approaching. His smile faded a little and he began to get up from the table. "I apologize, Director Mitchell. I have some things to discuss with the captain. We can continue our talk this evening."

"Alright, I look forward to it."

"So do I," Devaney nodded to Gavon as he quickly walked out of the cafeteria. The young professor just watched him go then shrugged. He was curious as to the reason for the cleric's attempts to avoid him, but he certainly wasn't upset about it. As far as he was concerned the less he had to deal with the Bishop, the better.

"Hello, Dr. Stills." Linus seemed to be in a cheerful mood.

"Hello Director, I have some questions about some equipment we seem to be lacking." Gavon responded after letting out a small laugh and turning to face the director.

"What do you mean? Everything is taken care of." Linus looked a little bit puzzled.

"I believe you, but we seem to be missing a snow cat and a couple of snow mobiles. Without them we are going to have a hell of a time bringing a half ton grizzly bear back to the ship."

"Of course, we are loading them once we stop for more supplies in Anchorage. It was quite a bit cheaper to pick them up there, as opposed to shipping them from Alaska to California, then taking it back to Alaska again."

"Fair enough. Well, I guess I don't have anymore questions about the equipment. Mind if I join you to finish lunch?" Gavon asked

"Very well, but don't you usually take lunch with Lynn and Logan?"

"Yes, but Lynn is going over the proper way to take ice cores with her class. And Logan is working on an experiment that will take all day."

So the young professor sat down and actually had a pleasant lunch with the director. Mitchell even listened to his concerns about the church's real motives for sending the monks and Father Devaney on the expedition with them. It was almost as if the two were friends. This was the first time in a long time that Doctor Stills had been pleased with the way things had been going with the director.

As the young professor was getting up from the table Logan casually walked up to him, glanced at Mitchell, and simply said, "It's time." Then he proceeded to walk off in the same casual manner.

Mitchell's mood, which had been relatively tolerable to this point, immediately went south. "Time for what?" he demanded. His disdain for Logan was very transparent.

Gavon looked at the director and simply asked a question. "Do you know why he enjoys messing with your head so much?"

"Because he's an ass hole," Linus said flatly.

"I won't argue that, but it's not the reason why you are his favorite target."

"Why then?" Mitchell demanded.

"Because you try so hard to avoid being human," Gavon said evenly.

"What is that supposed to mean?" He sounded angry.

Gavon replied with another question, "Well, when was the last time you had any real fun?"

"And what is your idea of fun Dr. Stills?"

"Well, the dictionary definition of the word is something along the lines of something which causes enjoyment. So when was the last time you did something solely for enjoyment? When was the last time you engaged in a hobby, read something that didn't have to do with work, or attended a party?"

Mitchell replied indignantly, "I was at the departmental fundraiser last month, you saw me there."

Gavon sighed, "That hardly qualifies as a party. I am referring to the kind of affair where there is no agenda, where people can drink and socialize without having to worry about whether or not they are talking to the right people to further their careers. I mean the kind of party that gets good when someone finally passes out in a ditch or dances naked on a table. And the police are sent out to break it up before ten o'clock at night."

Linus looked almost horrified, "I hope that sort of thing is not what you and Logan are planning."

Gavon looked surprised, how could Mitchell have found out about their plans for the next evening.

The director smiled a little, "Yes I know about the little gathering you are planning for tomorrow evening."

Stills hesitated for a moment and realizing that there was no point in pretending that he had no such plans, he sighed and asked. "How did you find out?"

"Brother Samuel told me, he overheard you and Logan talking about it a few days ago. That monk has a remarkable sense of hearing. It's pretty amazing."

This surprised Gavon even more than the fact that Mitchell had uncovered their plans. He was certain that he would have seen the monk if he had been anywhere close to him when he was discussing things with his friend.

He quickly composed himself and asked Mitchell, "So how are you going to handle it?"

"How do you think I am going to handle it? You are in violation of the rules of this voyage. I am telling you as your boss that if this little party of yours takes place, both you and Logan will be punished." Doctor Stills realized that there was something that Mitchell genuinely enjoyed after all. It was power.

"I figured you would say something along those lines. But I think that if you do something like that, you will be missing a great opportunity."

"What do you mean? My job is to enforce the rules of the university." Linus looked a little confused at the fact that Gavon was not only admitting to their plans, but was trying to talk him out of doing his job.

"For one thing, we are not breaking any university rules. We are breaking rules of the church, which have no place on a scientific expedition if you ask me. Secondly, you could gain some respect among the students and maybe even Logan. And all you have to do is act like a real person"

"Why do you think that?" Linus looked skeptical.

"If you show up to the party, everyone will assume you are there to break it up."

Mitchell laughed, "As it should be."

"However," Gavon continued, "Once they have reacted, you should do what they least expect."

"What would that be?" He asked.

"Simply walk in, get a beer and start socializing. At first they will be pretty confused, but it won't take long for everyone to warm up to you."

"Alright Gavon," this was the first time Linus had ever addressed him by his first name, "I'll play it your way. But I have to tell you I am not much of a drinker and I don't particularly like beer."

Gavon Smiled, "That doesn't matter, just showing up and trying to get to know everyone will go a long way. I'll see you there." With that Gavon walked off smiling. He had actually convinced Linus Mitchell to act like a human being. He chuckled to himself and wondered what Logan would say.

Chapter 7

"WHAT!!!!???" His friend's reaction was almost exactly what Gavon had expected it to be. Logan paced around the small room muttering something about the world coming to an end and throwing his hands up in dramatic fashion. "What's next, honesty in politics? Or maybe people in Mississippi will forget the civil war."

"I'm impressed honey," Lynn laughed. Her eyes showed that she really was.

"How did you convince him not to be a wanker?" Logan asked abruptly. "I mean that is like convincing a fly not to eat dog shit. It's just his nature." He continued to pace around the room still muttering to himself. To an outsider it would appear that Logan was not in his right mind. But since Lynn and Gavon already knew that fact and were comfortable with it, they paid little attention to their friend's antics. He wasn't even really paying attention to his friends by this point, he was simply too stunned by the news. Finally he sat down in a nearby chair, closed his eyes, and began rubbing his temples.

"I guess it's just my boyish charm."

"How much did you pay him?" Logan asked. "If you paid him off, you have to tell me. It may be quite a useful bit of information to have."

"I'm sure Gavon didn't bribe the director," Lynn laughed.

"I didn't threaten him with physical pain either Logan." Doctor Stills looked squarely at his friend, who was opening his mouth to say something, but just as quickly closed it.

"I've got it! He wants to sleep with you. That can be the only reason. That wicked little hobbit is finally coming out of the closet!" Logan quickly sat up in his chair. He was apparently was just talking, not listening. But finally Lynn's voice seemed to bring him back into the conversation.

"Linus Mitchell is not gay Logan," Lynn smiled. She was certain of this because of his unsuccessful attempts to pursue her before Gavon had come into the picture. He had taken her to lunch a few times, which she really didn't think much of since they were colleagues. But as soon as he sent her flowers, she had explained that she did not think that it would be a good idea to see each other as anything other than friends. He had apparently taken it well, but when Gavon came onto the scene he had become more unfriendly than usual. But that had apparently settled down after a few months.

"Then he must be either drunk or stoned. Mushrooms, that must be it, he's on shrooms, or some other Hallucinogen. He probably thought you were a giant, talking spider or something. I think I'll go find him and try to get a raise before he sobers up." Logan jumped up and pretended to move to the door. This brought a roar of laughter form Gavon and Lynn.

"I guess we had better finish preparing then," Lynn said, the smile had not left her face. "We are apparently going to have another guest at the party tonight."

"A fine idea, let's get to the cargo hold. I'll get Lance and Steve to help me carry the beer. There's quite a bit of it." This time Logan really did get up and open the door. "I'll meet you there in the hold in about half an hour, make the most of it."

"We will." Lynn Smiled as she closed the door behind him.

And they did.

Chapter 8

About an hour and a half later Lynn and Gavon showed up in cargo hold two. Logan looked at them as they opened the door, glanced at his watch, laughed, and shook his head. But he understood that they hadn't had a lot of time alone together lately. He was helping Lance and two other grad students, Dave and Lori move a large crate to the side of the spacious hold.

Dave was a slightly overweight biochemistry graduate student from Wisconsin. He had a plain face with a few freckles and copper hair. And in spite of being under the instruction of Doctor Fry, he was quite laid back. The truth of it was that he actually was one of the few students who did not really like Logan. The only reason he was studying under the crazy Englishman was the fact that he was such an amazingly brilliant scientist. Dave on the other hand did not have half of the natural ability of his teacher, so he had to study constantly. It annoyed him that Logan seemed to be able to grasp just about anything after reading it one time. But in this case he agreed with his teacher. The whole group needed some entertainment.

Lori was a slim moderately attractive woman from Florida. Her perky disposition more than likely came from growing up in close proximity to Disney World. She had come to West Tangiers to pursue her master's degree in Biochemistry. Unlike her counterpart, she genuinely liked Logan. His antics never ceased to make her laugh. In fact, the young had met her teacher as he was trying to find a good place to put an insanity alarm in the director's office.

The wonderful little device looked like a small box with a light sensor on top. When the light was on, it did nothing. But as soon as the light was turned off it began to buzz. He had hidden this contraption in Linus' office and then watched for about half an hour while the frustrated director turned the light off, heard the noise, turned the light back on to find the source. But since the light triggered the device to go silent, he had to stay an extra half an hour, getting more and more annoyed by the minute.

Logan had even laughed when there was a crash and a long sting of curse words coming from the director's office. The fact that it meant that his little toy would never function again didn't seem to bother him. He just watched as Linus deposited the device, now in very small pieces, into a nearby trash can. Needless to say, Lori had never had a professor like him before.

The cargo holds on board the Perseverance were quite spacious and had ceilings nearly twenty feet high. But other than the large volume and high ceilings, they looked no different than any other cargo hold. The walls were steel and no attempt had been made to hide the support beams or pipes, giving the walls a ribbed and veined sort of look. The ceiling was ribbed with the same kinds of support structures, as well as two long tracks near the sides for the door to move along as it opened. At one time they had been used to transport large quantities of goods to some of the most treacherous ports in the northern hemisphere. For this voyage the hold would serve as a make shift holding pen for a grizzly bear so that it could be observed more closely. However until that point it would serve as the perfect place for the professors and students to blow off steam.

"Nice of you two to join us," Logan yelled.

"Something came up," Lynn replied.

"So to speak," Gavon added.

Everyone laughed and continued to make space in the hold. After about an hour the room was as ready as it would ever be. The beer was cleverly hidden in a refrigerator that was marked for blood specimens from the various arctic animals to be studied as well as a number of coolers hidden in crates around the room.

This room had worked out perfectly for their purposes. The crates along the walls provided plenty of places to sit and the open area in the center provided an area for the undergrads to dance. A small stereo system sat inconspicuously on top of a box near the door, and a large crate with a few smaller ones around it would serve as a makeshift card table.

After one last look, the group was satisfied. This would be a welcome surprise for the undergrads. To this point they had been kept in the dark about it.

Chapter 9

Gavon finished his lecture on the differences between the Rodents and the Lagomorphs. As the students began to gather their things and get up to leave, he stopped them. It was time to tell them about the party.

"This is going to be a long and uneventful voyage until we get to our research area. In order to break the monotony, Dr. Fry, Levandusty and I have arranged a bit of entertainment for everyone. Tonight there will be a late night study session, at least as far as Father Devaney is concerned. It will be a chance to socialize and have some fun. Refreshments in the form of barley and hops flavored soda will be provided, but it would help if you would bring something to drink out of. The party will take place in cargo hold number two. I will see you all there."

Gavon then walked casually out of the room while the students talked quietly among themselves. In another classroom Lynn gave her students a similar speech. Logan, however, was much more straight-forward in his announcement.

"Alright my bright eyed, innocent little knowledge seekers, it's time to corrupt you. Tonight there will be a gathering of sorts that is sure to piss off our brown robed overlords, a fact that I personally take a great deal of pride in. Anyway, you are all invited to cargo hold number two for a night of revelry. As a further treat for all of you classes for the next two days are cancelled. If all goes well, you will need that time to recover anyway. I know I will. So I hope to see you all there tonight. We will get things started sometime after your evening feeding."

Logan then left the students in order to begin preparations for the evening. As he walked he smiled to himself. He was almost hoping for a confrontation with one of the clergy, and he got it.

"So Dr. Fry, corrupting the youth are you." The voice came from an obese monk named Brother Jonathan. His soft pudgy features were in sharp contrast to his piercing black eyes and wicked smile.

"No I'm not. I am simply letting them have a little fun. But I guess that is something you wouldn't know much about. Try it some time, you might like it." Most people would be a little annoyed by the monk trying to intervene in things that didn't have anything to do with him. But Logan was the kind of person who would never pass up the opportunity to have a laugh, particularly if it was at the expense of someone he didn't like. So he just smiled and faced the clergyman.

"As you well know alcohol is forbidden on this voyage," the monk said coldly.

"Of course I know that. But that doesn't mean I give half a shit. I'm aware of all kinds of silly rules that you would have all of us follow, but I don't care about those either. They seem designed to prevent people from having fun and nothing else. What do you people have against enjoying life anyway? Did you have very unhappy childhoods, or what?"

The monk started to respond, but Logan continued. "I mean aren't there monks in the world who brew beer in their monasteries? But you seem to think that if a person is having a good time, then it must be a sin. If you want to live like that, go ahead. Once again, I don't give a shit. But leave me the hell alone about it."

The monk was visibly annoyed and somewhat stunned by this point. "You should watch how you speak to God's earthly representatives, someday there will be judgment."

Logan laughed out loud. "Forgive me if I don't hold my breath. You people have been saying things like that for two thousand years. Besides I don't view you as representing anyone other than the Catholic Church. I definitely do not view you, or your brethren, as representatives of God. Any deity I would believe in would have to have some sense of humor. I mean look at the platypus or Ross Perot. If there is a god then there has to be some sort of divine joke book that is responsible for them."

"You openly reject the true word of God. Why would you do that?" The monk tried to look confused, but was unable to hide his obvious hatred for the man he was speaking to.

"It's quite simple really. I deny your assumption that you speak the word of God. I thought I was pretty clear about that. I mean do you really think that your religion is the first one to believe that it is absolutely right in its beliefs? Give me a break, every religion that has ever existed has had people who are absolutely convinced that they are on the one and only path to God. But then something else comes along and there are people who are absolutely certain that they are right and those of the older religions are wrong. Hell most of the time, they even start killing each other. Can they all be right?"

The monk opened his mouth again but again Logan continued to talk. "Of course not, so what makes your belief system any more valid than the one taught by Mohamed, Buda, or even George Lucas?"

Brother Jonathan looked intensely at the Englishman for almost a minute in complete silence. It was as if he was trying to burn a hole through him with his gaze. But when Logan simply yawned and looked at his watch, the monk looked a little surprised and then spoke evenly. "We offer answers to the most important questions. They are the ones that are not answered by people like you."

"Oh really, I have questions that I guarantee your religion cannot answer." Logan now had what could only be described as a shit eating grin on his face. He absolutely loved debating religion with people who were overly pious. He especially enjoyed punching holes in the logic of those who insisted on trying to convince people to believe what they believe, even when the potential convert had never expressed any interest in such things. If they would just keep their beliefs to themselves, then there would be no issue.

The truth of the matter was Logan couldn't really care less about what people believed. He just wanted to be left alone about it, much like Gavon. But, being the kind of person he was, he could not resist messing with someone's mind every time the chance presented itself.

"If it is something having to do with your scientific work, then I am not enough of an expert to answer," the monk said angrily.

"I know that, you probably would have a hard time telling me why certain elements are more reactive than others." His voice had assumed a deliberately condescending tone. "This question has to do with what is supposed to be your realm of expertise."

"What would that be?" Jonathan asked skeptically.

"How about the nature of God?"

"Yes, that is something that I have studied intensively," The cleric responded confidently.

"I figured that. So tell me this. In your belief, God is completely good. Correct?"

"Yes," the monk answered and began to wonder where this was going.

"Alright, God is all powerful. Yes?" Logan smiled a little more.

"Of course he is."

"So he created everything?"

"Yes," Jonathan was getting more irritated. How long would this annoying man continue to ask such stupid questions?

"Okay, based on what you just told me answer this. If God is completely good, all powerful, and created everything, then why does evil exist?" the professor asked triumphantly.

The monk stood dumbfounded, but Logan continued before he could say anything. It almost looked as if he was in the middle of a lecture in a classroom, since half of the class had gathered around to watch. "Absolute good cannot, by definition, create evil. So there are only a few possible answers to that question. One, that God is not completely good. Two, that God is not all powerful. Or three, God does not exist. So tell me which is it?"

The monk was silent for a moment, as if thinking of an answer. Then he spoke. "I truly feel badly for you, what is it like to live in a world without faith?"

"I have faith. But it is in things that can be proven, not simply because someone told me when I was a child that a man walked on water and was raised from the dead."

Now Brother Jonathan was looking squarely at Logan again. "People like you don't believe because they don't want to believe. That will change soon enough."

"Now that was quite possibly the most moronic argument I have ever heard." Logan adopted a more theatrical tone, as if he was an actor in a play. "By that rationale I should believe in the tooth fairy. After all I would like it to be true. In fact by my calculations she still owes me a couple of bucks"

The monk was now clearly getting angry, and Logan was enjoying it. "I am going to tell Father Devaney about this and about your plans for the evening. He might decide to turn this ship around and call this whole thing off."

With that the monk stormed off and Logan laughed. He knew that there was no chance of the bishop turning the ship around. After all, the church had its reputation at stake. To call off the expedition now would mean that the church would have to admit that it had been wrong, something that it had never been willing to do.

Logan chuckled again. Putting the monk in his place had made him feel very good. He casually walked down the narrow corridor, whistling softly to himself. He was curious to see what Gavon and Lynn's take on this little conversation would be.

Chapter 10

Several students had been nearby when Logan's encounter with Brother Jonathan had taken place. They all simply stood quietly looking on as their professor ripped into the monk. One of them, a brown haired girl named Stephanie, let out a snicker. She had witnessed Logan's performances several times, and they never ceased to amuse her.

The monk forcibly pushed his way past the four students and stormed down the hallway. After he was far enough to not notice, all of them broke out into laughter. Dr. Fry, or Professor Logan as he preferred his students to call him, was easily the favorite professor of all four. He seemed to really care about his work and the students. In addition to this he was more down to earth than most of the other professors at the university, even if he was more than a little odd. Aside from Professors Stills and Levandusky, Logan was the only professor who was frequently seen at the bars and clubs close to campus that were considered student hang outs. He would even by a round of drinks every so often.

The four began to speculate on what the night would bring.

"I'll bet he managed to smuggle an entire bar on board," laughed Stephanie.

"No, maybe some kegs, that's more his style," replied Kumar, a senior from India. His parents owned a large shipping company, so they were able to afford the high tuition for an international student.

"I wonder if Dr. Mitchell knows about this," Carl, a brown haired junior from Tennessee, pointed out. He tried to suppress his accent, but was unsuccessful.

"I doubt it, you know how straight laced he is. And I think that the most likely thing is that Dr. Fry managed to get beer on board without telling Mitchell. He is British after all. I just hope that it's some of his home brew," replied a shorter woman with curly blonde hair, named Lisa.

"He brews his own beer?" Carl asked in a somewhat surprised manner.

"That makes sense. But how did you ever taste it?" Stephanie asked.

"My boyfriend, at the time, and I had to drop off our research papers at his house once. When we got there we found Professor Logan, Doctor Stills, Doctor Levandusky, and a woman who turned out to be Dr. Stills' sister sitting on the front porch drinking beer and talking about where to go on vacation. Logan insisted that we try some of it. So we did, and it was possibly the best beer I have ever tasted."

"Wait a minute, why would you have to turn in a paper at his house, and not in class like the rest of us?" Kumar demanded.

"We were going out of town, and I wanted to turn it in before we left, rather than after we got back. Just so it would be out of the way."

"Oh, Okay. That makes sense."

"Well, what did it taste like?" Carl asked. He tried to look relaxed, but talking to Lisa always made him nervous.

"It was a lot like Bass Ale mixed with Shiner Bock, but maybe with a little more kick. I think that it has more alcohol than normal beer. It's probably closer to being a barley wine come to think of it."

"I guess it will probably be dark beer then," Carl moped.

Lisa leaned over and kissed him on the cheek. "Oh, I'm sure that you'll survive. I guess we had better go get ready. Come on Steph. See you boys tonight."

Then the two women left Carl and Kumar and hurried down the corridor to the women's dorm chattering about the evening ahead.

Kumar caught Carl staring at Lisa's backside as she walked off and said, "Why don't you just ask her out already?"

"What?" Carl whipped his head around to face his friend.

"You heard me. It is quite obvious that you would like to be more than just her friend. Just ask her out already."

"I can't. What would a girl like her want with me?"

"I think she likes you."

"Why would she want anything to do with a guy like me? I'm just a redneck from Tennessee and she is a sophisticated New Yorker. We don't have much in common. Besides, ask her to do what? We are on this ship, it's not like I can take her to a movie or something."

"I think you have more in common than you think. You just need to be more confident. Just walk up to her tonight and ask her to dance."

Carl looked terrified, "I don't know how to dance very well."

"Perfect, ask her to teach you then." The Indian smiled.

"Does that actually work?" Carl asked.

"I've used it on more than one occasion. I think that it is your best bet."

"But you're a great dancer."

"Exactly, it works. Trust me on this."

"Do you really think that I have a chance?"

"Yes, but you will never know until you try. Let's go, I'll give you some pointers while we get ready."

"Alright, thanks Kumar."

Then the two departed. Carl had no idea that Lisa and Stephanie had had a similar conversation on the way to their dorm.

Chapter 11

Brother Jonathan stormed into the room and slammed the door behind him, his disgust blatantly apparent. Father Devaney looked up from his writing, and faced the incredibly annoyed monk. After a few moments of watching Jonathan pace around the room trying to gain control of his emotions, the bishop spoke.

"Is something troubling you Jonathan?" He asked.

Jonathan glanced over at him as if to say, "What do you think?"

"Let me guess. Professor Fry?"

"How did you know?"

"I've seen people like him before. He is one of those people who think that religion is for the simple minded: a way to keep control of a populace that is too stupid to know right from wrong."

"Isn't that what it is essentially?" The monk asked.

"To most, but to those who truly know, it is the way to speak to and serve God."

"He asked me things that I couldn't answer. I think that he enjoys angering people like us." Jonathan was still clearly angry.

"His intellect and contempt for the divine make him, and those like him, very dangerous for the church. They must be convinced to stop speaking out against us. That is the purpose of this trip, remember?"

"So we need to make him one of us?"

"Yes, he needs to be converted," Devaney stated evenly.

"What about the others? Dr. stills, Dr. Levandusky, Mitchell, the students?"

"If they can be converted to our cause, so be it. If not, that is fine as well."

"I guess you know what they are planning for this evening. Don't you?" Jonathan asked.

"Of course, I know everything that is going on here." The bishop smiled.

"Are you going to stop them?"

"No. How much beer could they possibly get on board? I think we should let them drink through their supply and that should be the end of it." The older man looked back down at the documents in front of him.

"How long do you think that will take?"

"Not long. All of the students and professors drinking should insure that the beer flow has been stopped long before we get to our destination." He replied without looking up

"I hope you are right, it could certainly complicate things, especially if the crew gets a hold of it." Jonathan looked concerned, but he was calming down.

"True, but I don't think it will."

The two heard a knock at the door and stopped speaking immediately and watched the door open slowly. But when Brother Samuel waddled into the room, the pair relaxed again.

"Hello Samuel," Devaney said cheerfully.

"Hello Father. The crew will be running some practice drills tonight as you requested."

"Excellent. All professors and students should be below deck. So they should be out of the way."

"You were counting on something like this weren't you?" Jonathan asked.

"Of course, I would not expect a bunch of atheistic scientists to do as I say. Let them have their fun, in the end they will see that we are right."

"What about Fry?" Jonathan asked. "He's different than the others somehow. I tried to get some kind of insight into his mind, but he wouldn't reveal anything. I think that he'd hiding something."

"Everyone is hiding something." Devaney answered calmly. "I've gotten the same impression from the other two professors. People who have higher IQ's tend to have things in their lives that they would rather people like us did not know about."

"Are you admitting that they are smarter than we are?" Jonathan now looked surprised as well as angry.

"No of course not, but they think they are. But they are definitely not stupid."

"I think that there is something else going on with Fry. Something I'm not sure about. You have more experience with this sort of thing. I'd feel much better if you went with us, instead of leaving once we get to Anchorage."

"I agree with Jonathan." Samuel looked concerned and glanced at the door to make sure it had stayed closed.

"I understand your concerns, but you both are going to have to learn to function without me. I have instructed you to the best of my abilities."

"I still don't feel like I'm ready for something like this. What if something goes wrong?' Jonathan looked over at Samuel.

"I agree with him Father." The other monk turned to the bishop.

Devaney sighed. "How much trouble could they be? Besides the crew will be doing most of the work. Do you have any concerns that they will not listen to you?"

"No, of course I don't. But there could be problems. I don't like those trip leaders either. They could be trouble."

"You are going to worry yourself straight to your grave. If something comes up, you will have to deal with it. I have faith in you. You are my best students." Devaney smiled at the two of them.

"We still don't have the skill or experience that you do." Jonathan knew that the conversation was about to be over, but he felt he had to try.

"Look, the only way to get experience is by doing. So, both of you are going to have to do this without me. That is part of the reason for this trip. I won't be around forever. We will need people to take my place, the Cardinal's, and even the Pope's. Completing this assignment will prepare you for other greater things. So do what you are told and deal with the fact that I won't be here with you." Devaney then smiled again. The old cleric had been the mentor for the two monks for years. He felt they were ready to handle something like this. It was true that he had far more experience and training. But he felt that they needed to handle this on their own. "Let's talk about something else shall we?"

Jonathan sighed. "Alright, since we are apparently going our separate ways, where will you go next?"

Devaney sat back in his chair. "That is up to the Cardinal. But I would like to go back to the Mediterranean again. The Greek Isles are beautiful."

"Hopefully some day I will get to see them. But I haven't even been to Rome yet."

Samuel nodded in agreement with Jonathan. Neither of the two monks had ever been to the Vatican, or even met the cardinal Devaney was referring to. But both knew of him, and that he was really the one who was in charge. In fact this whole expedition had been his idea. They also knew that he was not the sort of man who liked being disappointed.

"Someday, you will, I'm sure of it. But in the mean time, take care of the business at hand." Devaney's voice sounded cheerful, but commanding.

"We will," the two said in unison.

Devaney smiled in a way that made the other two men uneasy. "I know you will."

Chapter 12

Logan merrily walked up to Gavon and Lynn, who were sitting near the bow of the ship with Malcolm and Quintus watching the sun set and discussing the evening's festivities. It was bitterly cold, but the fresh air made it worthwhile. Especially since this was one of the last sunsets they were going to see for a while. Lynn was sitting in Gavon's lap, with his arms around her. Quintus and Malcolm were on opposite sides of the couple, trying not to look uncomfortable.

"Well, isn't this romantic. The four of you look so cute like this. It makes me want to get in there and snuggle with all of you."

Lynn looked up at him and asked, "Why are you so cheerful, have you been playing with Mitchell's mind again? Or did one of the monks fall overboard?"

"Actually, I've been quite kind to the director lately, well for the past few hours at least. But I just had a wonderful discussion about theology with one of the resident experts. Jonathan? Yes, that was his name."

"Christ. How pissed is he?" Gavon asked.

"Very. But it's his fault. He really should have some clue about what he's debating before he opens his mouth. I simply pointed out one of the many holes in his rather ridiculous belief. He actually scoffed at the idea that the teachings of George Lucas are just as valid as those of the Pope."

Malcolm let out a quiet laugh and shook his head. Quintus rolled his eyes and went back to looking at the ocean. Then Lynn spoke.

"Logan, having beliefs in and of its self is not a bad thing. It brings comfort to a lot of people, and some religious organizations do a lot of good things. I hope you understand that."

"I know that, but he did start it. If people would just stop evangelizing then things like this wouldn't happen. He told me I was corrupting the youth. I just put him in his place." Logan paused and then casually added, "Which reminds me, they know about the party."

"What?" Gavon asked as if he had just been awakened by an alarm clock that had been set for the wrong time. Everyone else looked quickly at Logan.

"Don't worry about it. They won't do anything," the Englishman said casually.

"You sound pretty confident. How do you know that?" Malcolm asked.

"Has the church ever been quick to admit it is wrong?" Fry asked.

"No, I guess not," responded Malcolm.

"Exactly, if they ever do admit that this was a bad idea, it will probably be a couple of hundred years after we are all dead. I mean how long did it take them to admit that the Earth went around the Sun, not the other way around?"

All four of the listeners laughed at this. After all it was true. To call off the expedition now would require the Catholic Church to admit it had made a mistake, and they all knew that was pretty unlikely.

"So I guess we will continue as planned," Gavon stated.

"Logan. Who is handling the music?" Lynn asked with a raised eyebrow.

"Well, I will be bringing my CD's of course. But if anyone wants to bring something else, feel free. But nothing that sucks. Or you will be thrown overboard, along with your shitty music."

"And what you mean by that?" Quintus asked.

"The normal qualifications, no gangsta' rap. Did I pronounce that correctly? No Kenny G, and for fuck sake no Michael Bolton."

They all laughed again, and Gavon spoke up, "I think that we can handle that. I take it you will bring your Metallica collection?"

"Of course, we have to have some high quality music. I also have some Korn and Black Sabbath. But if you want to bring some country music so you can do that two stepping thing from your homeland, I will try to tolerate it as long as possible. But if you start line dancing I will have to administer a beating."

"Thanks, I guess." Gavon laughed.

Logan smiled, then paused and looked at his watch. "Well, I'm going to get a quick bite to eat. Then make my way to the cargo hold. I've heard that tonight they are serving mystery stew and Spam sticks. Does anyone want to join me?"

"Sure, why not." Gavon replied, and the group made its way to the cafeteria.

Chapter 13

Carl and Kumar entered the male dormitory and saw the other students preparing for the night's festivities. Some were discussing the beer that would be provided. A few were talking about what the lectures had been in the day's classes. But most were speculating on how the female half of the student population would be dressed and what their prospects for the evening were.

Carl walked to his bunk and slumped down on it. Kumar looked at him and said, "Just walk up and talk to her, you are already her friend. What is the big deal? Just ask her to dance or something."

Carl looked terrified, as if Kumar had just told him there was a fire on the ship.

"What?"

"I lied a little bit earlier. I can't dance at all. How can I tell her that? She will just laugh at me." He then began looking intently at his shoes.

"For one thing I don't think that she will laugh at you. Just get her to teach you. Or, if that is too much pressure, take a walk up on deck with her. Women like that sort of thing. She's far more interested in who you are than how you are going to try to entertain her tonight."

Two other students standing close by heard this and walked over. They were the only two on the ship of African decent and were named Gerald and Robert.

"Maybe we can help you," Gerald half said and half laughed.

"Do you think my situation is funny Gerald?" Carl asked without looking up.

"What? No, I'm not laughing at you. I'm laughing at how stereotypical this situation is. I mean it's kind of like a scene from a bad eighties movie."

"No kidding," Robert cut in, "I mean a white guy who can't dance getting help from a couple of brothers. The only thing that could make it better would be if Kumar was wearing a uniform from a gas station."

"I do know how to make a Slushy, you know," Kumar laughed.

"I'm glad you find it amusing," Carl sighed.

"Very amusing, but I still want to help you." Gerald looked at the young man from Tennessee.

"Alright, what do I need to do?"

"Well, first of all I need to know what I have to work with. Let's see some of your moves," Gerald instructed.

"My moves? What do you mean?"

"He means dance monkey boy." Robert laughed.

"But everyone is watching." He was right. Everyone had stopped getting ready and had begun watching the small group.

"Not quite everyone, none of the girls are here, and they're the ones you are going to be trying to impress. Who cares what these clowns think of you." Gerald gestured to the group of onlookers.

"Alright, but remember I grew up in Tennessee."

Then Carl began moving in a way that best resembled a duck with a broken wing and only one leg trying to run on a frozen pond.

Robert slapped his hand over his mouth and ran out of the room as fast as he could. He was followed by several other students. From the hallway there was the sound of hysterical laughter that would begin to subside, only to start all over again, much like the tide during a storm.

Carl looked at Gerald, "I know I'm hopeless."

Kumar had his hand over his mouth and his eyes were watering. All he could manage was a nod of his head and something that sounded like a weak cough as he tried to suppress the laughter welling up inside him.

Gerald, amazingly, was able to speak, "It's not your fault. I've seen this thing before. I'm sorry to be the one to break this to you." He sighed and put his hand on Carl's shoulder as if he were a doctor about to give someone some really bad news. He then took a deep breath and looked Carl squarely in the eyes. "You just have an incurable genetic disorder."

"What?" Carl didn't expect him to say anything like that.

"You have W.B.R.D.S. unfortunately there is no cure."

"What the hell is that?" Carl looked concerned, after all Gerald had given up a baseball scholarship in order to focus on his pre-med degree, which he now had a 4.0 GPA in. So Carl figured he knew what he was talking about.

"My friend, it's a horrible disease that affects millions of men. It stands for White Boy Rhythm Deficiency Syndrome. I'm so sorry, but there is nothing that can be done for you." Gerald's voice was as even as it had ever been. So it took a few seconds for Carl to realize what he had just been told. "I might be able to get you in touch with a support group, so you don't have to face this alone."

Kumar couldn't contain himself at that point and began laughing so hard he found it hard to breathe. Finally he caught his breath enough to speak. "Well, I guess dancing is out of the question." He coughed. "You'll have to try talking to her."

"But I don't know what to say." Carl seemed strangely apathetic about the laughter at his expense. He had expected it, so that had softened the blow a bit.

"Just be yourself." Gerald told him.

"I guess I'll have to," Carl sighed.

"Look, probably the best thing for you to do is to get her to take a walk with you. You will probably be less nervous if it is just the two of you," Kumar advised in a slightly broken voice.

"How do I get her away from her friends?"

"Leave that to me," Kumar smiled.

"Thanks." Carl was beginning to look a little more confident.

"We should probably get there before they do. It will give you a chance to get a drink or two into you. Maybe that will help your nerves a bit."

"Good idea Gerald," Kumar responded.

"Alright, let's finish getting ready then," Carl agreed.

Chapter 14

Lisa hadn't shut up about Carl since the voyage began. So, Stephanie, as good of a friend as she was, was tired of hearing it. But she simply stood there and listened as always.

"Look, why don't you just throw all of that traditional crap out the window," Stephanie finally said.

"What?" her friend sounded surprised.

"You keep waiting for him to make the first move. He's not going to."

"He's just a little shy," Lisa responded.

"Yes he is. But you may be waiting a long time for him to get up the courage to try to move your friendship to the next level."

"I know, but I don't want to push him." Lisa sighed.

"If you don't then nothing may ever happen."

"And if I do, it may scare him off."

Stephanie laughed. "First of all he is a 21 year old heterosexual male, so an attractive woman paying attention to him is definitely not going to scare him off. Secondly if you don't say something to him soon, I will. If, for no other reason, it will make you shut up about him. You are driving me nuts."

"Sorry I guess I have been talking a lot about him. He's just not like the other guys. I mean every other guy I've met since high school has been trying to do one thing, get into my pants. But Carl actually seems to want to know me."

"I'm sure he wants to get into your pants as well," Stephanie replied.

"Probably, but I don't care. He seems to want to get to know me. And I think he actually means it. I think that the two of us could have something resembling a relationship, not one of those one night stands that we've all had."

"Maybe you're right. He does seem to be of a higher caliber than most of the horny frat boys back at school. I certainly don't miss having to deal with them," Stephanie reflected.

"No kidding. I once had a Sig actually sit next to me at a party and start talking to me."

"What's so interesting about that? It happens to me all the time."

"He then proceeded to throw up on one of his buddies and pass out in my lap."

Stephanie laughed, "Well, I guess that's one way to get in between your legs."

Lisa laughed too. Carl was definitely not that sort of guy. Maybe in high school the two women would have been interested in how much a man could drink. But now they were much more interested in what kind of person he was. And Carl was certainly different.

He was a bit shy, that was obvious, but he was also a very caring kind of person who'd stand up for his friends no matter what happened. That fact alone went a long way toward impressing Lisa. But there was also an innocent sort of charm about him. Lisa smiled at her friend, just as another woman stepped out of the bathroom wearing a towel.

"Well, it looks like the shower is free. So I guess we'd better get ready. You can go first. I'm going to do some thinking."

"Alright, but don't fantasize about him too much. You'll see him in an hour or two." With that Stephanie picked up a towel and went to get in the shower. She looked back at her friend, laughed a little, and shook her head. Lisa was clearly excited about the evening. It would certainly be one she'd never forget.

Chapter 15

Gavon and Lynn entered the cargo hold shortly after finishing dinner. Not surprisingly Logan, Lance, and Steve, along with two other grad students named Rick and Mark, were already drinking and playing cards.

Lynn looked at her lover as if to say, "Go ahead honey."

Doctor Stills gave her a kiss and asked, "Do you want to play too?"

"No, I'll just watch. Besides, you're going to end up with all the money anyway."

They both knew that there was very little doubt that the young professor was going to win anytime he played cards. He'd actually used his poker skills when he was an undergrad to help pay his bills. To Gavon it was like a chess game, except that the people involved were playing for money. It was all about tricking the opponents into making mistakes. And in the case of no limit it only took one mistake to go broke.

Most people simply thought that it was all luck. But the professor from Texas knew differently. So he looked over at the game and laughed a little bit. Then he turned back to Lynn and smiled at her.

"We'll see. I won't take all night."

"Just have fun." She smiled and kissed him.

"Alright, but let's get a drink first." He motioned to a nearby cooler. The pair got their beers and then walked over to the group playing cards. Gavon smiled when he saw that they were playing Texas Hold 'em, the game that had helped him pay his way through undergrad more than any other.

Mark laughed as he won a fairly large pot, but as soon as he looked up and saw Gavon his mood changed.

"Shit. I guess you want to play don't you Dr. Stills." His face was reminiscent of a puppy that had just been caught peeing on the rug.

"As a matter of fact I do," Gavon replied as he sat down and put a couple of twenties and a ten on the table.

"I tell you what, why don't you just kick me in the nuts and take my wallet, then we can call it a day," Mark said with an air of sarcasm in his voice. This comment created sporadic laughter among the members of the group even though they knew the man had a point. Within a few minutes, the game has started anew. Gavon settled in for a nice game as Logan dealt the cards. It was a much lower stakes game than he was used to, but it was friendly. After all nothing would be friendly about playing for thousands of dollars even if the opponents were practically family.

The money didn't matter to him. It was much more of an ego thing. The truth of it was he planned to give their money back to them anyway. Even though he had once been a cutthroat poker player, he would still feel bad taking money from his students. The young professor remembered being in school, and how fifty dollars was a lot back then.

But he wasn't going to tell them that, at least not until he'd seen them sweat a bit. It was one of his guilty pleasures. Watching people become more and more nervous filled him with a kind of childish glee. It had been that way since his teens.

By that point in his life he had turned his back on everything his parents had taught him, and had begun to run with a crowd they certainly would not have approved of. His friends had been involved in various criminal acts, and as a result Gavon had learned many of the skills that people would not expect to find in a college professor.

But he'd realized that by the time he was leaving for college, that there was no future in that life. So, before he was caught, he'd left it behind and become a successful student. College had given him a chance to reinvent himself. So he had tried to keep his head down and do his work. Although some of the things he'd learned would always be part of him.

Gavon stretched his back and popped his neck and then took a look at the first two cards he was dealt. His face didn't show it, but inside he was dancing a jig as he looked down at two aces.

Chapter 16

The first undergrads to arrive at the party were Ryan, Gerald, and Carl. Kumar and Robert showed up about two minutes later. It was pretty apparent that the young man from Tennessee was very nervous. His friends had given an enormous amount of advice, but he still didn't know what he would say to Lisa when she finally arrived.

Kumar and Ryan were the first students to find the beer and the others quickly joined them. Carl greedily downed his first cold one. But when he started to reach for a second, Kumar grabbed his hand.

"You don't want to be dead drunk when she gets here you know."

"Sorry, I'm just kinda' nervous." Carl put the beer back in the cooler.

"Don't be. I'm sure that she feels the same way about you too. Besides, you don't want to be acting like a fool, so take it easy with the bottled stupidity. That sort of thing may work for some ditsy sorority chick. But Lisa is much more interested in who you are. So are the other girls here for that matter. And you are not some drunken frat boy. So just be yourself."

"There is just so much to be nervous about." Carl looked back at his friend.

"What do you mean?"

"Well, for one thing I am about to try to make a move on the coolest girl I have ever met. On top of that we are at a party drinking with three professors. Combine that with the fact that the people in charge of this ship would certainly not approve of this and might come barging in any time. What is there to worry about?"

"Well, other than that I mean," Kumar laughed.

Carl just rolled his eyes. He could feel the effects of the beer already. Certainly Dr. Fry had managed to increase the alcohol content much higher than he was used to. Kumar was probably right, he should hold off on getting another one for a while.

"Remember what we told you Carl. Just stay calm and try to be yourself. But don't think of it as making a move. Just think of it as a pleasant conversation with a good friend. Then just see where it goes." Gerald told him. "Oh, and for fuck's sake don't try to dance."

"I'll try, thanks again guys. You're good friends."

"Oh, you're going to make me cry," Kumar laughed.

Robert then tapped Carl on his shoulder. "Show time," he said as he motioned towards the door.

Carl turned around to face the group of girls entering the room. But to him there was only one, Lisa.

"I may need help," Carl said to Kumar.

"No problem, we can run interference for you."

Chapter 17

"Shit!"

Lance and Rick stood up at the same time and threw their cards on the table. Gavon smiled and casually turned over his cards, pocket queens which gave him a full house. Lance and Rick had drawn a straight and a flush respectively which were just big enough to lose all of their money. Gavon laughed a little and pulled all of their remaining chips over to his stack. Lynn smiled, leaned over and kissed him.

"Horniest hand in poker." He smiled.

"How's that? Rick asked.

"Whenever it's played, it always screws someone," The professor laughed.

They all laughed a little at Doctor Stills' comment and Logan began to deal the next hand. His chips were dwindling, but since he knew his friend better than the students he had managed to avoid some of his traps.

"Looks like it was a threesome in this case," Rick said as he shook his head.

"Well, thanks for the lesson professor," Lance laughed.

"Yeah, but someday one of us is going to beat you," Rick added.

"I'll be waiting," Gavon smiled back.

"Come on let's get a drink, I certainly need one." Lance slapped Rick on the back and the two began to walk towards the nearest cooler.

"I think I'll join you boys," Lynn said. "Come on, I'll buy."

"Thanks Lynn," Lance laughed, "Your man should have been a professional card player. Is there anything he isn't good at?"

"Well, chalk it up to a misspent youth. If you really want to beat him at something, try sports, football, baseball, or basketball, anything like that." Lynn said.

"What?" They both said in unison.

"It's true, he has no clue about the sports world," Lynn laughed. "I can even throw a football better that he can. It's actually quite funny."

"So you are telling me that someone as fit as Dr. Stills doesn't follow sports?" Rick sounded genuinely surprised.

Lynn laughed a little. "No, he can tell you all of the differences between a nutria-rat and a muskrat, or the probability of a five-six off suit beating pocket aces before the flop, but he couldn't tell you who played in the Super-Bowl last year. I guess it's one of the many things I love about him."

"Interesting, I guess you learn something new everyday," Lance stated.

"So what kind of childhood did he have? I mean my dad pushed me to play baseball, football, and hockey," Rick asked.

"Not Gavon. When his friends were out playing baseball or football, he was looking under rocks and logs for critters, or he had his nose in a book. Besides he and his parents haven't ever really gotten along. So even if his father had pushed him to be a jock he wouldn't have listened."

"Why don't they get along? I mean, if you don't want to tell me anything that personal, I will understand, but I am curious. I just haven't seen Gavon ever get upset at anyone. Why wouldn't he get along with his parents?" Rick looked genuinely confused.

"His family is very religious, psycho-Christian conservatives, as he calls them. Don't get me wrong, Gavon doesn't hate all Christians. But he doesn't believe it personally. In fact he doesn't care what people believe as long as they leave him alone about it, he's just a little more low-key about things than a certain Englishman I could mention."

"So, if he doesn't care what people believe, then why don't they get along?

"It's because they do. Religion is such a big deal to them that when Gavon decided it wasn't for him, they didn't know how to handle it. His parents kept on trying to push him back into their belief system, but he kept resisting. Finally when he left for Cornell, he thought that his parents had come to terms with his decision. He thought that maybe they would start treating him like an adult." Lynn paused for a moment and looked across the room at her lover. Two more students were sitting down at the card table for a lesson.

Then she continued, "But he was wrong. They simply changed tactics. His parents kept trying to trick him into going to church events and things like that. After a while he got really tired of it and quit asking them to stop. This time he told them to."

"Was that the end of it?" Lance asked.

"It was for a while. But then they started again. Finally he was fed up and told them not to contact him anymore. I have only met them once. When we went to see his sister, they showed up. I think she put them up to it. But it was just more of the same."

"That is a pretty sad story. I would never have guessed he would have cut off contact with his parents." Lance said dreamily, "But I definitely understand, my parents don't accept me now, my father in particular."

"Well, if he hadn't, he never would have studied so hard to get his doctorate."

"He's in awfully good shape for a bookworm," Lance pointed out.

"You have no idea," Lynn grinned. "When he was a teenager he got interested in martial arts and rock climbing. That may have a little to do with it."

"I knew he was a climber, but I never knew he was a fighter too." Rick sounded surprised. "Intelligence, strength, and speed, but he hates sports. Odd."

"He doesn't talk about it much. I guess he doesn't consider it something that he needs to tell people all the time. But I once saw him bring a huge guy to his knees without throwing a single punch."

"How do you mean?" Lance asked.

"We went out into the Texas hill country one time looking for fossils. One night we went to a little bar for a drink. It was the kind of place Logan would get into trouble in. Things were going pretty well until Gavon went to get a couple more drinks, and the line was apparently pretty long at the bar. While he was gone this huge guy came over and started to harass me. He looked a lot like Bluto from the old Popeye cartoons." Lynn Stopped and laughed a little bit then she continued.

"I told him that I wasn't interested, but he still wouldn't leave. He kept trying to grab me and pull me onto the dance floor. When Gavon came back he also explained that we were together, but the man still wouldn't back down. He put the drinks down on our table and the man grabbed him by the shirt and pulled his fist back." Lynn laughed and took a drink.

"What happened then?" Rick asked. He and Lance looked like a couple of wide eyed kids listening to a story about some mythical hero.

"I can't say exactly, it happened too fast. But the man never got a chance to swing. The next thing I knew he was down on his knees whimpering like a little girl. Gavon had pulled his middle finger back and made it touch his forearm."

"Ouch," Rick said and tried to see how far he could pull his own finger back to replicate what Gavon had done.

"No kidding. It gets better believe it or not. After he made the man apologize to me, Gavon made him apologize to the whole bar for being an asshole. Then he made him buy a round for everyone."

"No way," Lance blurted out.

"Yep, he really did. Finally when Gavon released him the man actually thanked him." Lynn laughed and looked adoringly back across the room at her lover.

"Why?" Lance half asked and half laughed.

"I don't really know. I guess it was for not killing him. After Bluto left, Gav sat down and acted like nothing had happened."

"Are you making that up?" Rick asked.

Lynn shook her head. "It was one of the most amazing things I have ever seen."

"I guess Dr. Stills doesn't scare easily does he," Lance pointed out.

"No he doesn't, I've never seen him even shaken."

"Well, I'm certainly glad I'm on his good side," Lance laughed.

"I wouldn't worry too much about it. Gavon is not a violent person. That is the only time I have ever seen him come close to being in a fight, he usually doesn't even raise his voice."

"Well, I need another beer after that," Rick laughed.

"Good idea," Lance joined him and Lynn walked back over to where Gavon was sitting, and put her hands on his shoulders.

He looked up at her and smiled, "Why are you so happy?"

"Just glad that I have you."

"Me too."

Chapter 18

Lisa, Stephanie, Jaime, and two other girls named Dana and Tracy walked in just in time to see Gavon relieve Rick and Lance of their money.

"It looks like Professor Stills is still teaching," Jaime laughed.

"Well, well look at this. The boys are all dressed up tonight. They almost look respectable." Dana pointed out.

It was true. All of the male students were dressed in the best clothes they had brought on the voyage. Which were far from Armani suits, but the gesture was appreciated. The five girls looked at the group of guys and knew it was going to be an interesting night.

Lisa noticed that Carl was watching her exclusively, but when she caught his gaze he quickly looked away and began talking to Kumar, trying intently to seem uninterested. She smiled a little and knew that he was trying to work up the nerve to walk over and say something to her.

Stephanie turned to Lisa, "I think he may just work up the courage this time."

"I hope so," Lisa responded.

"He will," Stephanie smiled, "Kumar won't let him back out now."

Stephanie had known Kumar for a couple of years. The two had had several classes together and had eventually become friends. The young Indian seemed more American than many of the students who had lived in the U.S. for their entire lives, if his accent could be overlooked. The young woman had spent several hours one night talking to him about India and it had become apparent that he liked life in the states much more than in his homeland. For one thing there wasn't much chance of Canada or Mexico attacking America. But in India there were always concerns about Pakistan lobbing a nuclear warhead across the border.

Technically he was a Hindu, but he was not a very devout one. Kumar had told her that he really did not believe in the supernatural. Like many people his age and of his intelligence, shortly after he had begun his education he had begun to ask questions, in a similar manner as Gavon had. But since religion could not answer these, it had begun to have less of an effect on his life. By the time he was eighteen he had turned away from his family traditions completely. He still had respect for the beliefs of his culture but had realized that they were not for him, which kept him on good terms with his parents. But he still had rejected religion wholesale.

Stephanie had been entranced by the stories of his youth. She had told him how they were a stark contrast to her childhood in Baltimore. Kumar's family was extraordinarily wealthy and lived on an estate in southern India. From the large patio of the enormous house it was possible to see the ocean. It fascinated her that that Kumar's family had a group of elephants, much like American ranchers kept horses.

By the same token he had been fascinated in even the simplest aspect of American childhood. He had always wanted to go to a Yankee's game. The idea of sitting in the stands watching the great American past time and eating a dirty water dog was a dream he had always had. The two had been planning to go to New York in the coming summer. At some point Kumar planned to take some of his friends, including Stephanie, to his family's estate in India. He was even going to take them to a nearby river to look for rubies and sapphires.

After a while the two had become very good friends. Kumar had even gone with Stephanie to visit her family over the winter break. Despite her father's initial objections, Kumar had managed to charm her whole family. He looked across the room at Stephanie, who was saying something to Lisa, no doubt concerning Carl. But as soon as she saw him she nodded. The young Indian smiled back at her, it was show time.

Chapter 19

Carl realized that he was walking toward the group of girls even before it registered that Kumar had given him a good shove to get things started. He let the shy man take a few steps. Then he laughed a little and followed his friend, Carl may need saving after all. But from the Indian's perspective, he seemed to be doing fine.

The two made their way to the group as Gerald and some other guys from the dorm looked on. Gerald and Robert, shook hands, but not in a way that seemed congratulatory for a job well done. They seemed to be making an agreement. Fortunately Carl did not know that they had actually made a wager on whether or not he would go down in flames.

The young man from Tennessee walked with a determination and his mind became clearer than it had ever been. A wave of absolute calm engulfed him as he approached the most perfect woman he'd ever met. Her smile and light green eyes seemed to draw him into a world that was empty, except for the two of them. He was actually doing it, he was about to be alone with the most wonderful person in the world.

Then it happened. Somehow a piece of ice had fallen on the floor from one of the coolers. Unfortunately it happened to find its way directly under Carl's shoe. He stepped down on it and felt his foot begin to slide out from under him. The sensation immediately ripped him out of the wonderful world he had fallen into and back into reality.

The young man found himself sliding uncontrollably towards the group of girls. His other foot, the one that did not have a slippery piece of coldness beneath it, was lagging behind him. Carl realized that he was about end up doing the splits. "Good job Carl, really great first impression," he thought as he slid towards what he knew was going to be incredibly painful.

The desperate young man moved his foot forward and tried to regain his balance, and for a moment Carl thought that he'd been successful. But then, to his horror, he started to spin. His eyes widened as he saw Lisa's reaction. She knew something was wrong, and looked concerned. This actually brought a small amount of comfort the man from Tennessee. It would have been even more demoralizing for him if she had been laughing like everyone else. Carl quickly realized that there we only two options. The young man could try to stop the spin, which would almost certainly cause him to fall, or he could simply ride it out. He chose the latter.

Carl made a complete pirouette and came to a stop in front of a very surprised Lisa. The young man stood there for a moment trying to figure out what had just happened. He was still swaying a little, and in an effort to keep his balance he bent at the waist. To everyone present, it appeared that he was actually taking a bow.

Everyone stopped laughing and was silent for what seemed like an eternity to Carl. Finally he felt a hand on his shoulder, it was Kumar.

"I thought you said you couldn't dance," the Indian said loud enough for everyone to hear.

Carl simply stood there trying not to look terrified. But then he looked at Lisa, expecting her to be laughing. Instead she was smiling at him. Before anyone else could say anything or laugh at him she spoke.

"I'll have to say that you just made the best entrance I have ever seen." Her warm smile helped to steady his nerves a little.

Carl looked back at her and tried to think of something to say. But it was Kumar who spoke instead. "Well, he didn't want to make that sort of introduction, but I made a bet with him that he couldn't do it." As if to emphasize this, he handed Carl a twenty and patted him on the back.

"Thanks," Carl whispered to his friend. Then he looked back at Lisa, who was still smiling and moved closer to her. "So, nice party," he said. In his mind he was cursing at himself. "So, nice party, that's the best you could do? You jack ass."

"Yes it is," she responded. Lisa then looked at the assembled group, and realized that everyone was staring at them. "Why don't we get a beer?"

"Sounds good to me," he agreed as he noticed that all of his friends were watching them and whispering to each other. So the pair quickly turned and walked to the nearest cooler to get some refreshment.

Chapter 20

Carl and Lisa went to get drinks for the group and began talking.

"You look nice tonight," Carl managed to say in a surprisingly calm sounding manner. It was a much easier to talk to her without everyone else standing there studying his every move.

"Thanks, so do you." She hadn't stopped smiling yet.

"This is crazy. Don't you think?" He was starting to feel a little more comfortable.

"Why would you say that?" She asked.

"What if Director Mitchell finds out? Don't you think the professors will get into trouble?" He sounded concerned. Carl didn't like the idea of his three favorite teachers getting disciplined for doing something nice for the students.

"I don't think they really care. We're all stuck on this ship for a while with nothing to do. I guess they figure that we need something to break the monotony or we'll go insane." She looked at Professor Stills, who was still at the card table. "Besides none of them look terribly concerned about it."

"I guess not," the young man laughed as he watched Professor Fry and two students participate in a chugging contest, which Logan easily won. He then realized that he was talking to her and he was not at all nervous.

Kumar had been right. Carl handed Lisa a beer and she smiled at him again. He realized that she felt the same way about him as he did about her. Now as long as he didn't do anything stupid, things should begin to progress nicely. Maybe they would fall in love and get married some day. That thought made Carl feel good. This girl from New York was everything he had always wanted and more. The somewhat romantic young man had never been the kind of guy who stopped the fantasy at the bedroom scene. In his mind it played out the whole way. It was a little odd for a twenty one year old college student to think that way. But this was one of the reasons she liked him so much.

"Thanks, I can take it from here." Her voice snapped him back into the present. Carl realized he had handed her the beer, but had failed to let go.

"You're welcome," Carl responded with a slightly shaky voice. He then looked at his friends who had begun mingling with their female counterparts. All of them were watching the couple intently, but trying hard not to let them notice. But then he saw Robert drop his head and stare at the floor for moment, then hand Gerald what looked like a twenty. "Those bastards are betting on how I'll do," he thought.

"Do you ever feel like everyone is watching you?" Lisa asked.

"Yeah, all of the time lately," Carl laughed.

"Do you want to get out of here?" she asked seductively.

"What?" Carl half choked on his beer.

Lisa patted him on the back to help him clear his lungs. Then she looked deeply into his eyes and he knew that she was serious.

"Come on, let's take a walk. Maybe we can get away from all of these spectators before they start placing bets." She reached out, took a hold of his hand, and began to lead him to the door.

The young man coughed again and nodded, apparently she hadn't seen Robert hand Gerald the money. So the couple moved casually to the door. Carl managed to catch a glance at Kumar who gave him a thumbs-up and pretended to wipe a tear away from the corner of his eye.

As the two made their way out the door, Kumar turned to Gerald. "Well, that wasn't exactly how I hoped it would play out. But I guess he made an impression."

"Yep, I guess our little boy is finally all grown up." Gerald then put his head on Kumar's shoulder and pretended to cry. "I'm so proud of him."

"Oh knock it off you two." Stephanie was standing in front of them shaking her head. "Now that the drama is over, do any of you clowns want to dance?"

"Alright, come on ladies, this is a party." Gerald grabbed Jaime's hand and led the surprised young woman to the dance floor. The rest of the group followed suit and before long no one was talking about Carl and Lisa.

Chapter 21

Malcolm and Quintus arrived just as Carl and Lisa were leaving. The Australian looked at his friend as if to say, "That was quick." But the other man simply shrugged and continued into the room.

"Well it looks like things are getting started," Malcolm pointed out.

"So they are. Not to change the subject, but I've been wondering about something." The southerner said.

"What would that be, mate?"

"Is Logan insane?" He gestured to the Englishman, who was doing what appeared to be the Mexican Hat Dance around a Bunsen burner near where Gavon was sitting, while a small group of students watched and laughed.

"I wouldn't say insane, I'd say he is crazy."

Quintus turned and looked at him. "I'm sure that there is some subtle difference in your definition of those two terms. But in my world they are pretty damned close. So please explain to me what that is, my Vegemite eating friend."

"Well, an insane man has no idea what he is doing. Logan knows full well what he is doing, he simply doesn't care. So in my estimation he is crazy, not insane." Malcolm laughed.

Quintus shook his head, "Somehow I doubt that is the clinical definition."

"Call it what you will, but that's how I see it. And remember, you asked."

"Hmmm, I don't think that he is the only one who's crazy," Quintus nodded as he took a shot from his flask.

Malcolm laughed again, "Probably not. Well, I suppose we had better say hi to everybody."

"I guess so." The two adventurers made their way into the room, but it wasn't long before a familiar, and obviously drunk voice rang out.

"Malcolm, Quintus, you are just in time for an age-old tradition," Logan shouted to them.

Malcolm smiled and walked over to where Logan was standing. Quintus looked a little confused, then shook his head and joined the two. He was wondering what this age-old tradition was, when he felt a gentle hand grasp his arm. It was Lynn.

"I hope they aren't going to do what I think they are going to do," She said, sounding a little worried.

"And what would that be darlin'?" Quintus asked.

As if in answer to his question there was a roar of laughter and cheering from where Logan was standing. Malcolm quickly joined him and the two jumped up on top of a couple of crates followed by Lance and Rick.

The crowd cheered as Logan shouted, "Are you ready for Singing in the Rain?"

Quintus looked at Lynn, who rolled her eyes and shook her head.

"Well, I'm sorry to say that that was what I was afraid of," The blonde woman sighed. Then she and Quintus walked over to Gavon, who had looked up from his game, and was watching with an amused look on his face. "You aren't going to let this get out of hand, are you?"

Gavon looked at Lynn and smiled, "Do I ever?"

Lynn looked back at him skeptically, but said nothing.

"Alright, alright, I won't let him go overboard. But you have to admit it is pretty funny." He laughed a little bit.

"I'll grant you that. Just make sure he keeps it in the PG-13 range at the most." Gavon started to open his mouth to say something, but she stopped him with a kiss. Lynn then stepped back and smiled. "If you are a good boy, maybe later I'll give you a reward."

Gavon smiled back, "Well since you put it that way, I'll stop him if I need to."

Lynn leaned over and kissed him again, then walked over to talk to Samantha, a senior geology student with long dark hair from Pennsylvania. Gavon watched her go and thought about the fact that there was nothing that he wouldn't do for her. Then he smiled again and continued to watch his friend make an ass of himself.

Chapter 22

Linus Mitchell entered the room that was once a cargo hold, and gazed upon a sight that he would never forget. Logan, Malcolm, Lance, and Rick were standing on top of a row of boxes singing "Singing in the Rain." This by itself would not be terribly disturbing, although none of them could carry a tune. But in between repetitions of the verse, Logan was shouting something and the others were repeating.

After the first verse Logan yelled, "Hold on!"

"Hold on," the group repeated.

"Wait a minute!"

"Wait a minute!"

"Shirts off!"

"Shirts off!"

Then the four proceeded to take off their shirts and throw them to the crowd of cheering students. Mitchell was horrified. The possible repercussions for this were severe indeed. The potential sexual harassment lawsuits, the scandals, and worst of all, it all could come back on him. After all, he was in charge. The short man also began to think about what might happen should Father Devaney come walking in. Such a sight could cause the old priest to call off the whole expedition, or possibly have a heart attack. Linus wasn't sure which would be worse.

This could mean the end of his career, and of course it would be the fault of Logan Fry. All of these thoughts were frightening enough to the director. But his horror intensified as the group finished the next verse.

"…what a glorious feeling singing in the rain."

"Hold on!"

"Hold on!"

"Wait a minute!"

"Wait a minute!"

"Belts off!"

"Belts off!"

As the group burst into song again, Linus knew he had to do something to stop this before it got any more out of hand. But there was really no way for him to get to the group since the cheering crowd surrounding them was as dense as a mangrove swamp.

He could simply yell at them to stop and break up the party right here, but then the director thought about what Gavon had told him. If he did that, then the lonely man would never gain the acceptance he so desperately craved. But this thought was somewhat irrelevant as Linus had never had a loud voice and any protest he made would certainly be drown out by the roaring crowd. The short man had to find a way to stop them without coming off as someone opposed to people having a good time. But how could he do that?

Mitchell realized that his best hope would be to somehow get Gavon's or Lynn's attention. He began to jump up and down waving his hands. This made him look a great deal like a leprechaun. But this motion was overlooked since Linus was significantly shorter than most of the students, who all had their hands in the air cheering.

"Hold on!"

"Hold on!"

"Wait a minute!"

"Wait a minute!"

"Trousers off!"

"Trousers off!"

The group then stripped their pants off, twirled them in the air, and threw them to the now intensely cheering crowd. Mitchell might have been impressed by the degree of coordination the group showed, if he hadn't been so disturbed by the whole thing. Then just when he thought and that they were finished and began to let out a sigh of relief, they began singing again. The director knew he had to do something and quickly, Gavon's advice be damned. The short man began to run towards the group but was unable to fight his way through the wall of cheering students. As soon as he got close the mob shifted and pushed him to the floor. The director quickly got back to his feet and shouted. But the noise from the students was deafening and he couldn't even hear himself as he tried in vain to get people to move out of his way. Then he was knocked to the floor a second time. This time he simply lay there as a wave of hopelessness enveloped him. The feeling of despair rolled over him leaving him in an almost trance-like state.

A couple of the students managed to turn around long enough to find out what they'd been bumping into. They quickly realized what had happened and with horrified looks reached down to help the small man back to his feet. He tried to wave his arms again in a half-hearted effort to get the attention of Doctor Stills. But the professor was pretty intent on his card game and didn't seem to notice. But as Logan and the others began to sing again, he saw the professor look up.

Fortunately for Linus, Gavon got up from his poker game and stopped the group before they could finish the final verse that would have certainly ended in "shorts off." Mitchell took a step back and let out a small sigh. Then he felt himself fall the rest of the way into a state of disbelief, as what had just occurred continued to sink in.

Professor Stills was helping his insane and now very inebriated friend look for his clothes when he saw the director. He was standing alone with a small number of students looking at him, then each other uneasily. The director's expression was something similar to what could be expected if a young Amish man was suddenly dropped off in Las Vegas. Gavon was pretty sure that Mitchell had just witnessed more that he could handle. Linus confirmed his suspicions by slowly slumping to the floor and sitting in silence. So he glanced at Lynn, who was a lot closer to the stunned director. She smiled at him, but quickly realized he was trying to tell her something. When her expression changed to a questioning one, the young professor motioned to Linus. Doctor Levandusky looked in the direction her lover was pointing, looked back, and nodded. Then she quickly made her way to the small, stunned man, put her hand on his shoulder, and began talking to him.

"Director Mitchell, are you okay?" she asked in a soothing voice.

Mitchell simply looked dumbly at her, as if she had been speaking in a foreign language.

Everything began to calm down a bit as the other revelers, one by one, began to notice the director. Gavon waded through the crowd and quickly joined his love and their motionless supervisor. Who looked at him and tried to speak, but all that came out was a low whimper.

"Director Mitchell, it's alright. Nothing happened that will cause the university any problems," Stills told him, it was as if he could read his mind.

Linus was beginning to turn pale and then said something that the pair would have never expected, "I need a drink," he said very timidly.

The pair smiled. Then Gavon shrugged as if to say, "why not?" He stood back up from his crouch and hurriedly went to get a brew for Mitchell.

"Now go easy on that stuff, it's a little stronger than most beers," Gavon advised as he handed the cold bottle to the stunned man.

Mitchell downed his beer with surprising speed and reached for the one Professor Stills was drinking. He drained that one as well without saying a word, and snatched a third from a nearby student. After a short time he began to loosen up a little. Some would say a little too much.

Chapter 23

Carl and Lisa walked along down the corridor leading to the upper deck. They heard the beginning of the "Singing in the Rain" episode and each laughed a little. Both had witnessed the spectacle and knew that it was officially a party now. She casually looked over her shoulder and when she saw no one there to heckle them she leaned against him and let out a satisfied sigh.

Carl was a little surprised, but his arm seemed to involuntarily wrap its self around her mid section as they continued to walk. He was nervous, but this was going well at the moment. The young man just hoped he could avoid doing something stupid.

The pair continued to walk toward the stairs and the noise from the party slowly faded. Once they were at the staircase, Carl took a step up, but then realized that Lisa hadn't followed. Instead the young woman took a hold of his hand and gave it a slight tug. This caused him to turn and look back at her to ask what was wrong. But before he could, she stepped forward and kissed him. He was surprised, but needless to say he didn't resist.

After their short embrace she stepped back and looked up into his eyes. "Wow. That was nice."

Carl couldn't speak, so he just nodded and sat down on the stairs. Lisa joined him and leaned her head on his shoulder again. The pair sat in silence for a moment while each thought about what was happening. Once he was certain that this was real, the young man finally spoke.

"Do you have any idea how long I've wanted to do that?" He asked.

She laughed a little. "Probably about as long as I have."

"Really?" Carl looked surprised.

"I've had a thing for you since we were lab partners in Biology 101." She responded.

"That was two years ago. Why didn't you ever say anything?" Carl asked.

"I guess I was waiting for you to make the first move. But you never did."

Carl sat there for a few moments trying to figure out what to say. But then she leaned over and kissed him on the cheek.

"I don't think that it's a bad thing that we never got together until now," she said.

Carl laughed this time. "Why would you say that?"

"Well, it's given us a chance to get to know each other. I mean if we had just jumped right into bed, I might not have ever gotten to know who you are."

Carl looked shocked, "What?" Her straight forward, New York manner still caught him off guard sometimes.

She smiled back at him, "I think it's better to base a relationship on something other than sex."

Carl Still looked like he had just been slapped, but not necessarily in a bad way.

"Oh, don't worry. You're going to get laid tonight," she said evenly.

"Did you just say what I think you did?" He looked straight at her.

Lisa smiled back at him and nodded. Then she wrapped her arms around him and sighed. The couple sat there for a while just trying to absorb what was happening. It felt so good just to be with one another.

Finally Carl leaned over and was about to kiss her again, when he saw something move at the end of the hallway. The young man looked down the corridor and saw Director Mitchell walking slowly towards them. He then turned to Lisa and sighed, "Well I guess we aren't going to get any alone time here either. Are you still up for a walk?"

She smiled at him again and took his hand and they ascended the stairs hand in hand onto the deck.

Chapter 24

Linus had begun to feel strange. It had been a long time since he'd had more than one drink on any occasion. Strangely he felt like this was something he had been missing out on. All of the anxiety, and out right terror, he had felt began to melt away as the genie of the jolly juice wrapped him in her warm, comforting embrace.

He finished his third beer and reached for another one. By this time Gavon and Lynn had gone to have a dance. The director was apparently not going to have a break-down, besides a slow Clint Black song was now being played. Mitchell felt someone slap him on the back just as he was taking his first mouthful from the new bottle. This caused him to choke a little and squirt beer through his nose. As he bust into a coughing fit he heard Logan's voice.

"Sorry mate, I didn't mean to choke you. But if you have to go, drowning in beer is top of the list of ways I'd choose."

Linus turned around, still coughing, and looked at Logan. Fortunately the Englishman had his clothes back on, although his shirt was now untucked and he was swaying a little bit. Dr. Fry actually looked happy to see Director Mitchell. Which was not an uncommon sight, but this was different. Logan didn't look happy that his favorite target for joking was present and apparently vulnerable. The Brit looked happy to see someone he actually liked. The director couldn't remember the last time that he had seen Logan pleased to see him without something exploding shortly after.

"So what do you think of the ale?" Logan asked.

"It's good," the short man managed. He looked around nervously, still expecting something to blow up, or in some other way cause him to be the subject of one of Logan's pranks. But nothing happened, at least not immediately.

"It's my own recipe," Logan grinned.

Linus looked scared again. That must be it. That bastard had put something in the beer. What would it do to him? Maybe it would cause him to be sick or something worse.

Logan seemed to read his mind, "The beer's fine, maybe a little higher in alcohol than lesser beers. But it won't do anything bad to you."

"Are you just setting me up for something or what?" the director was skeptical.

Logan laughed and shook his head. "Not this time. I'm just glad to see you having fun for a change. Relax and enjoy yourself, you need it."

Then the Englishman sauntered off, leaving Mitchell to contemplate all that had happened so far this evening. The short man reclined on a nearby crate and after he realized that Logan really wasn't going to do anything cruel to him. He then did something that shocked some nearby students. The straight laced director smiled a genuine smile.

Chapter 25

Carl saw something moving out of the corner of his eye and quickly turned to look.

"What is it?" Lisa asked.

"I'm not sure, but I definitely saw something." Carl began to look around for whatever he'd seen.

"Maybe it was one of the crew," she offered.

"I guess it could be, but there was something not quite right in how it was moving."

"What do you mean?" she asked.

"I really don't know, but it didn't move like any person I've ever seen," he continued to scan the darkness.

"Let's get a closer look." The adventurous woman began to move toward the place where he'd seen whatever it was.

"Are you sure? What if it is some sort of animal, a bear or something?"

Lisa just looked at him and laughed a little.

"Alright, stupid question," Carl said. Of course it was a stupid question. The ship had been at sea for over three weeks now. How would a bear or any large animal get on board anyway? Even if one had, there would be no way it could have remained unnoticed this long. Carl shook his head, muttered something about his own idiocy and began to walk towards the last place he had seen the person. By this point he'd decided that it had to be a member of the crew, who was probably sick and needed help.

From a distance the man, they had decided it was a man, seemed hunched over as if having pains in his stomach. He was also walking strangely, like someone who had a sprained ankle. Carl assumed that he was trying to make his way to the rail of the ship, so he could puke over the side. The icy wind whipped across the young man's face and reminded him that they were much farther north now, probably close to Alaska.

Lisa tugged his arm, "We should help him. If he falls overboard in this he's as good as dead."

"You're right, as usual. Let's see if he needs help," Carl replied.

The couple started across the slippery deck towards the man, who had stopped and was now swaying back and forth while still somewhat hunched over with his back to the pair. The wind was so cold that it felt like it was burning their faces as they moved towards him.

Neither of them saw the frozen puddle on the deck. They were too focused on the sick man. Carl was the first to step into it. His feet slipped out from under him and he knew he was going down. Lisa caught him and tried to prevent him from hurting himself, but since the man weighed significantly more, he simply dragged her down with him. The young woman landed lightly land on top of the young man, and in spite of being a little winded, he couldn't help thinking about how good it felt to have her body pressed against his.

The pair lay there in silence for a few seconds, and just when he opened his mouth to ask if she was alright Lisa kissed him again. It wasn't a simple peck on the cheek like a friend would do. This was a lover's kiss, soft and slow. Both had forgotten the man they were going to help for the moment and everything seemed to be going so well. Then out of the darkness came an ominous voice, a man's voice. And he didn't sound pleased.

Carl and Lisa quickly looked up to see Father Devaney standing over them. The priest had a look on his face that matched the irritation in his voice. "I said, what are you doing up here?"

Lisa answered, "We were just taking a walk."

"It looks like you were going to do a lot more than that. Most people walk in an upright position," The old man responded.

"I slipped, and when she tried to keep me from falling, she landed on top of me. We were going to see if that man over there needs help. He looks like he is sick or something," Carl barked at Devaney, his concern for what kind of trouble they could get into was quickly overpowered by the realization that this man had just interrupted one of the best moments of his life.

Carl stood and helped Lisa to her feet. Then he turned to the bishop, who had just been joined by Brother Jonathan. The young man was furious now, it was apparent that these clerics were far more concerned with stopping the couple from committing what they viewed as a sin than they were with the welfare of the crewman behind them. The priests even seemed to deliberately move so that the view of the crewman was blocked.

The student couldn't help what he said next. "Why don't you get off your moral high horse and see if that man is alright, if he hasn't already fallen overboard. I am so sick of you people making an issue out of something that shouldn't be one. We are adults, and damn it we should be treated as such. Besides, don't you ass holes care about the sick man behind you, or are you so concerned with our immortal souls that you won't help a fellow person in need?"

Lisa was looking at him with a mixture of concern and admiration. This was a side of Carl she had never seen before. It made her feel proud of him for standing up to the priests. After all they should have been more concerned with the crewman, but they hadn't even turned to see him yet.

Jonathan took a step back, as if he was a little afraid of the angry student. But Devaney just smiled in a way that made him look a great deal like a demon. "You two should go back below deck. It is dangerous up here, besides you don't look well young man."

The priest was right, for some reason he did feel a little ill. His knees began to feel weak and he would have fallen down if Lisa hadn't held his arm to steady him. The man from Tennessee felt as if his very life was being drained from him. He looked up at Devaney and got the distinct feeling that the bishop's gaze was responsible. But then he realized that that was not possible in the real world, maybe he had eaten something earlier that was spoiled, or maybe it was the rocking of the boat. But food poisoning and sea sickness were well known to him, and this didn't feel like either of them.

His head began to spin and the world went black, the last thing he heard was Lisa's voice, sounding very distant, asking him if he would be alright. Then he slipped into the world of dreams…or nightmares.

Chapter 26

Lynn looked around the room, walked over to Gavon, and asked, "Where is Director Mitchell?"

Doctor Stills looked up from the table. "I don't know. The last time I saw him he was talking to Steve. I guess he might know."

"We should probably try to find him," she sighed.

"He's a big boy. I'm sure he can look after himself." He smiled at Lynn. But she didn't smile back so he quickly changed the direction of his conversation. "Alright, alright, I guess we should, come on." He turned his cards over, smiled at the two students who were left, and pulled the rest of his chips over to his side of the table. "Good game guys." He then joined Lynn, leaving the two students to sit and contemplate the odds of 5 7 of spades beating ace jack, and pocket nines in the same hand.

Gavon and Lynn walked over to Steve, who was now talking to Logan. The drunken Englishman offered a beer first to Lynn, then to her lover. But when they both declined, he shrugged and then began to drink it himself, in spite of already having one in his other hand.

"We may have a problem," Stills said flatly.

"What are you talking about? I think everything is going pretty well. Even the rat faced midget has cut down on his wankerisms." Logan laughed and finished his original beer. He looked around for a place to set the empty bottle and finally decided on a nearby crate.

Then he quickly looked at his friend as if he just realized what he was talking about. "The only problem I can find is the motion of the ship is preventing us from constructing a proper beeramid." Logan then tried unsuccessfully to stack the bottles on top of the crate. But after they fell for a third time he gave up and looked at the two other professors again.

"That is a pretty serious problem. But it isn't exactly what Gavon is talking about. Do either of you know where Linus is?" Lynn asked.

"Come to think of it he has been gone a while." Steve looked at his watch. "About half an hour, I wonder what's keeping him."

"He probably had to take a shit. Why are you so worried? If he's not here, then we don't have to deal with him." Logan swayed a little and began to laugh again. The alcohol was apparently taking more of an effect.

Gavon gave him a sharp look.

"Fine, fine, I'll help you find the little bastard. Steve did he say where he was going?" The drunken Englishman asked.

"Yeah, he said he was going to the restroom. He seemed a little drunk, maybe he passed out somewhere."

Logan began to snicker at the thought of Director Mitchell lying face down, drooling in a hallway somewhere. "Okay, let's go find him. But I insist that we at least bring a camera to allow the others to share in Linus' misery?"

Gavon looked at his Doctor Fry and then shook his head. Apparently he had given up on trying to get his friend to take this situation seriously.

"I'll stay here so there will be at least someone other than the students. If Mitchell showed back up and none of us were here I think that he might have a heart attack. I'd suggest you stay, Logan, but I think that seeing only you and the students being here, without adult supervision could very well cause his head to explode" Lynn said.

"That sounds like something I'd like to see. But, you're probably right, love. I guess I'll go with your man and help find the director." Then Logan smiled. "Besides, I would hate to miss seeing Linus in any kind of discomfort, especially if I may have a chance to shave one of his eyebrows."

"Keep an eye on Logan, sweetie," Lynn laughed. "You may want some more help as well."

"Good idea." Gavon motioned to Malcolm and Quintus to join him. After he explained the situation and allowed a moment to let the Australian and his British counterpart get over their laughter Doctor Stills began giving instructions. "Quintus, you and Malcolm check the restroom at the end of the corridor. Logan and I will check Mitchell's room. If he's passed out, we'll probably have to take care of him. He is our boss after all."

Quintus nodded and began to walk towards the door with Malcolm. After a quick kiss from Lynn, Gavon left with his English friend, who was still snickering.

The pair proceeded up one deck and down the narrow corridor to Director Mitchell's room. Logan seemed surprisingly quiet. But then Doctor Stills realized that he had not set down his beer before they had left the party and was still drinking it. The Texan thought about the headache it would be if one of the clergy were to catch his friend drinking. But since at least it kept him quiet, so he didn't say anything. When they got to Mitchell's room, Gavon gave a loud knock.

"Director Mitchell, are you alright?" he said rather loudly towards the steel door. When there was no answer, Stills looked at Logan. "Well, I guess we should go in."

"I suppose we should. But I'm not cleaning up if he's ralphed all over the place."

Gavon shook his head and tried not to let out a small laugh. It was somewhat humorous to picture someone as straight laced as Mitchell lying face down in a pool of his own vomit.

He opened the door and stepped inside. The room was immaculate, which wasn't all that surprising. Not a single piece of laundry was out of place. But the director was nowhere to be seen. Logan stumbled in after him and looked around. "Well, it would seem that Linus did not decide to go to bed, can we go back to the party now?" Even as he spoke, Doctor Fry picked up his supervisor's day planner, which was on the night stand by the bed, and stuffed it under the mattress.

Doctor Stills watched this with a certain degree of amusement and then spoke. "You just can't help yourself can you?"

His friend just smiled and shrugged. Any opportunity to torture Mitchell would never be passed up by the Englishman.

Gavon turned to Logan and was about to remind his friend that they needed to find the director before they returned, when he saw Malcolm stagger up to the open door. He had tears in his eyes, was holding his stomach, and could hardly stand. At first the Texan thought that something must be terribly wrong, but he quickly realized that the tears were from laughter instead of sorrow or fear. The Australian's face was even red and he was having trouble breathing.

The pair stood in the doorway looking at their companion. But the Australian was still laughing so hard he couldn't speak. He started to try to say something, but then burst into a new fit of uncontrollable laughter and fell to the floor. Malcolm lay in the hallway braying like a donkey for a few moments. Then he tried to get up, but only managed to make it to one knee.

Gavon and Logan continued to stand and watch him for a few minutes while he laughed uncontrollably while rolling on the floor and holding his stomach. Finally The Australian raised his hand and indicated that he needed a bit longer.

"Malcolm, did you find him?" Doctor Stills asked, he was a little irritated, but was becoming more amused by the minute.

The Australian nodded and then burst into a new fit of laughter.

"Malcolm, if Linus is in pain, I want to share in the experience," Logan attempted to sound stern. But when he snickered a little bit it was even more apparent that he wasn't annoyed with his friend at all.

"Is Director Mitchell alright?" Gavon asked, as he gave Logan a harsh look.

"Not really," the laughing man managed. Then he began again.

"Where is he?" Stills continued.

Finally, Malcolm managed to compose himself enough to stand. "Come on I'll show you, you've got to see this." He started back down the corridor still chuckling sporadically. Gavon looked at Logan, who simply shrugged and started following the Australian. Dr. Stills shook his head then followed his friend.

The Australian led the pair back to the restroom at the end of the corridor where Quintus was standing. Upon their arrival he looked up and then shook his head. Gavon realized that Linus was probably not in any danger since Malcolm was still laughing and the Georgian seemed relatively unconcerned.

The southerner looked at the Texan and simply said, "It isn't pretty. But you need to look for yourself. Then we can decide what to do."

Chapter 27

Quintus opened the door to allow Doctor Stills access to the small cramped bathroom. It reminded him of the kind you would find at a filthy little gas station in a small town in Texas. The floor was far from clean. Small bits of wadded up toilet paper were scattered about, a testament to the crew's idea of cleanliness. A small sink with what had been a mirror at some point adorned the wall to his right. Of course now it simply looked like a dirty sheet of steel hanging crooked on the wall. Just inside the door and to his left were two stalls.

"He's in the closest one," Quintus answered Gavon's question before he could ask it.

The young professor stepped forward with a sigh, preparing himself for something he was sure that he would find incredibly unpleasant. As Stills took another step forward, he heard a small splash. His boot was now in the middle of a puddle that he desperately hoped was water. Although he knew in his heart that it was something much more foul.

The smell in the place was almost unbearable. The odor of old half cleaned up urine was mixed with the unmistakable aroma of human feces and the overwhelming stink of fresh vomit. Gavon looked back at Quintus, who simply shook his head and let out something between a sigh and a laugh, then looked at the floor. Logan and Malcolm were standing behind him laughing. Apparently the Australian had shared the plight of Director Mitchell with his British friend.

The Texan knocked on the door, "Linus are you alright?" But there was no answer. He let out a sigh and began to slowly open the grimy door. What he saw inside was quite possibly the most disgusting, and at the same time hilarious thing he had ever seen.

Director Linus Mitchell, possibly the most uptight and boring human being on the planet, was sitting on the toilet with his pants around his ankles. This was disturbing enough since Big Jim and the twins were in full view. But it was even worse since Mitchell's pants were filled, much like a bowl, with chunky vomit consisting mostly of beer and half digested pot roast.

Gavon had the urge to throw up and laugh at the same time. What emerged instead was a coughing fit. He quickly staggered out into the hall to get some air. As the professor stood in the hallway coughing, he felt Logan push his way past him.

The coughing man finally was able to compose himself enough to hear his friend's commentary on Linus' condition.

"Oh, that's not right!" He heard his friend yell for inside the filthy little room.

"No it's not," Malcolm added before bursting into a new fit of laughter.

"Look, he had the presence of mind to put the lid up and pull his shorts down. How the hell did this happen?" Logan laughed.

"I don't know. I mean I've had to make some hard decisions in my day, but nothing like that." Malcolm responded in between bouts of laughter.

"Well, this is a first. I think that if I was in that situation I would probably decide to sit instead of kneel too," Logan said. "This may be the first time since I met the little wanker that I fully support his decision."

Almost as if to try to answer Dr. Fry, Linus groaned a little and looked as if he might fall off the toilet. But instead he leaned slightly to the side and came to rest against the grimy side of the stall, his head resting on the toilet paper dispenser. Logan let out a little chuckle as a thin string of drool began to escape the director's mouth.

"I don't know," Malcolm responded. "I mean yes, it would be hard to decide. But I think I might make the other choice. I think I could hide having a load in my shorts easier than a stomach full of half used beer and food. But I guess it really is a question of consistency."

"Consistency?" Gavon asked.

"Yes consistency. I mean are we talking chili or bread dough?"

"I'm not going to like where this conversation is going am I?" Gavon thought out loud.

The Australian continued, "I think that in the case of dough, I would make the opposite choice. But if it was something like chili, then I would agree with him. Should we look and see which it was?"

"That's disgusting you Aussie bastard." Logan laughed.

Malcolm simply looked at him and blinked.

"Fair enough, I don't really think that this situation could get much more unpleasant." Logan laughed. "Gavon, Quintus, what would you do in his position?"

Quintus laughed a little and shrugged. "I really have no idea. I also hope that I'm never faced with a situation where those are my only two choices."

"Gav?" Logan looked at his friend.

"I agree with Quintus, I hope I never have to make that decision."

"Well, I think that we all do. But if you had to, would you sit or kneel?" Doctor Fry continued to prod.

Stills rolled his eyes. He couldn't help but see the humor in this situation. And he knew that Logan wasn't going to let up until he got an answer. So the professor from Texas finally gave his friend his answer, "I guess I would sit as well. But I think I would at least try to spew to the side instead of into my shorts."

"Ha! I knew it, that's two to one Malcolm, you stinky bastard. I'll bet you don't wipe either do you."

All four laughed a little more at this. But after a few minutes the realization hit them that they were going to have to move Mitchell, in spite of his condition.

"So, how do you want to handle this?" Quintus asked Gavon.

"I think that we should charge an admission fee to everyone. So they can witness this spectacle until he wakes up. I think that 2 or 3 dollars should be fair."

"That is exactly why he didn't ask you Logan," Stills responded, he sounded a little annoyed.

"Malcolm, why don't you and Logan try to find some towels or something?" Quintus said. "That way at least we don't have to actually touch him."

"O.K. Malcolm, you get the towels, I'll go get the students," Logan then acted like he was going to run down the hallway to get the young people. But then he saw that his friend was not amused by his antics and sighed. "Just fooling around Gav, we'll find something and get back as quickly as we can."

Stills nodded and watched the laughing pair leave. When they were gone he turned to Quintus and laughed, "I'll have to admit, this is the funniest thing I have ever seen."

"Agreed, but I figured since Malcolm had pretty much lost control when he first saw the situation, I should contain myself to the best of my ability. I suppose you had to do the same because of Logan."

"Yeah, I usually serve as Logan's voice of reason. It's been like that since we became friends."

"You seem to be very much in control of your emotions Dr. Stills, that's an admirable quality, as well as a rare one." The Southerner pointed out.

"It's served me well I suppose." Gavon couldn't help but think that the southerner's comment was a little odd. "I'm guessing you know what that's like too."

"I've worked hard to gain this much control. My experience has been that the more emotion that goes into making a decision, the poorer that decision tends to be."

"Well put, I mean I would do anything for Logan and Malcolm, but could you imagine what would happen if they were in this situation by themselves?" The professor laughed a little.

Quintus shook his head, "I'm afraid that I can, it would be humorous, but not well thought out."

"There would probably be at least one explosion as well. But I think that Logan can actually take things seriously if he has to. He just doesn't like to."

"Malcolm is probably the same way. Hell, I have seen him at his best, and he can focus when he has to. I think both of them just feel that people like us take things too seriously, and maybe we do."

"Yeah, but I guess someone has to be serious."

Quintus chuckled, "Indeed. Well, I think I hear laughter. I wonder what they found."

Chapter 28

Lisa helped Carl back below deck. He was semi-conscious, but he could walk with help. She really didn't know what was wrong with her friend, but she was pretty sure that Professor Levandusky or Professor Stills would know what to do. The young woman wasn't entirely sure of what they had seen, but she knew that had been was strange. The New Yorker decided that once she got help for Carl, she would tell the professors that something weird was going on.

So many things were swirling around in her head that she almost slipped on the stairs leading down below deck. Devaney had just looked at the pair of them and told her to get him below deck. It was strange. The young woman hadn't asked if they would help her or anything. She'd simply obeyed him. Normally she would have been very irritated that neither the priest, nor the monk had offered to help her. After all Carl weighed about seventy pounds more than she did.

She shook her head in a way that a person who was trying to stay awake might do. Her thoughts began to clear and she suddenly became quite scared. As much as it didn't make sense to her scientific mind, she began to think that the bishop was able to manipulate people to do whatever he wanted them to do.

No, that didn't make any sense. There must be some kind of rational explanation for what had just happened. People were not able do that sort of thing, no matter what the science fiction writers might say.

Carl groaned a little bit and began to lose his stability. Lisa could tell that he was losing consciousness completely. So the small woman tried to walk faster. But by the time they reached her destination she was, by any reasonable standard, dragging him. Finally the exhausted woman reached the door to the cargo hold and was relieved to find that it was slightly ajar. Otherwise she would have had to set the young man down and turn the heavy wheel to open it.

Lisa stumbled into the room and immediately saw Professor Levandusky, who was apparently waiting for someone to come through the door. When she saw the pair, she hurried over in order to help. Before either spoke, the two women set the now unconscious Carl gently on the floor. The younger woman was breathing hard from the effort of carrying the heavier man down the stairs and through the hallway. She tried to speak, but Lynn stopped her.

"Calm down, just catch your breath and then tell me what's going on," Lynn said calmly as she knelt down to examine the unconscious student. "Start with what happened to Carl."

"I'm not sure. We were talking to Father Devaney and he just passed out." She then took a deep breath.

The professor looked at her as if to ask how much beer the young man had had to drink earlier.

"He's not drunk." Lisa answered before Lynn asked.

"Okay I believe you, but that thought did cross my mind. Did he seem sick at all to begin with?" She then looked back at the student lying on the floor.

"No, he was fine until Devaney showed up, but then he just got dizzy and fell over." She was still breathing hard, but she was recovering from the effort.

Lynn gently opened Carl's eyes and was stunned at what she saw. His pupils were expanding and contracting rapidly and independently, creating an almost hypnotic effect. She closed his eyes and sat back a little. The young professor had never seen this before and was a little confused.

"Is he going to be alright?" Lisa's voice betrayed the deep concern that she was feeling for the young man.

"I'd be lying if I said I knew. I haven't ever seen anything like this before." Lynn sounded concerned, "We need to get him to the ship's doctor."

The professor looked around and was faced with a difficult decision. Carl needed to get to the doctor as quickly as possible. But if she left, the other students would be left without any supervision. Doctor Levandusky looked across the room and found Steve. He hadn't been drinking very much. On top of that he was a very responsible person.

She motioned for him to come over to her. He quickly joined the two women and looked down at Carl, who was now lying on the floor looking like he was asleep.

Chapter 29

Gavon and Quintus deposited Linus in the shower, as Logan and Malcolm looked on and cracked tasteless jokes.

"So, who gets to do the honors?" Doctor Fry asked. "I mean I don't want to be the one to help take his clothes off. Seeing Mitchell completely naked might cause me to have nightmares for the rest of my life."

"Good point Logan," Gavon responded. "I think that we should turn the water on and see if it wakes him up, then maybe he can undress himself."

Doctor Stills reached into the small shower and turned the knob. Fortunately for the group, the cold water shocked the director into something resembling consciousness. He looked around groggily and then his eyes settled on Logan, who was wearing a comically large grin.

"What did you do to me, you sick bastard?" Linus managed to say, apparently unconcerned about the cold stream of water pouring over him.

Logan began to speak, but then his friend stopped him and spoke. "He didn't do anything to you." Gavon said calmly. "You just had too much to drink."

"I'm actually quite impressed." Not surprisingly, the Englishman was not able to stay quiet. "I mean you lasted a lot longer than I thought you would. But I think that I would have stopped before I was faced with that most unfortunate choice you had to make." As if to illustrate his point Doctor Fry turned his bottle up and finished the remaining beer.

This gave his friend the chance to speak again. "You might want to get out of those clothes and get a shower."

"I guess I should since I am soaking wet now." Mitchell sounded pretty irritated as he had just seemed to realize that he was fully clothed in a running shower.

Linus then stood up and seemed surprisingly stable, given his condition. He turned and looked at the two professors as if to say, "Do you mind?"

Logan opened his mouth, but shut it quickly when his friend elbowed him in the stomach. "Alright we'll leave you to it," Gavon said.

The pair walked into the hallway to join Malcolm and Quintus.

"Well, he's surprisingly aware of his surroundings. I have to give the little rodent credit. I wouldn't have ever thought he'd recover this quickly." Logan then laughed a little. "Can we go back to the party now? I am completely out of beer." He then turned his bottle up over his mouth again and tapped the bottom of it to get the remaining few drops of the dark liquid.

"I don't see why not. He will probably finish his shower and then go to bed. We can check in on him later."

"Good let's go see if anything interesting has happened while we've been gone."

Chapter 30

Rick, Lisa, and Steve helped get a half conscious Carl to the ship's doctor. It was slow going, and more than once the group had to stop when the sick man completely lost consciousness and became little more than a 200 pound sack of potatoes.

But after a difficult trek they finally arrived at the ship's clinic. Miraculously the doctor was in. Doctor Blain was a thin, twitchy man who had apparently had some kind of accident when he had been younger. There was a large jagged scar that ran the length of his right cheek and ended in a rather large triangular shaped crater near his jaw line. As interesting as this was, he never spoke about its origin. And no one ever worked up the courage to ask him. In fact most of the students thought that the doctor was somewhat creepy. But that was not something that was on Lisa's mind at the moment, she was only concerned with the well being of her friend.

The doctor took one look at the unconscious student and sighed, as if he were being bothered. "Bring him into the exam room and I'll take a look."

The group half carried, and half dragged their friend into the small room. Rick and Steve lifted the sick man onto the examining table and stepped back. The room was very small and with all four people standing around the table it was uncomfortably cramped. So the two men stepped out into the hallway to wait, while Lisa stood back and allowed the doctor to examine Carl.

He opened the unconscious man's eyes and looked at the strange behavior of the student's eyes in the same manner as a person might look at a traffic light waiting for it to change. Then Blain took his pulse and began to scribble something on a clipboard. Finally he looked at Lisa and spoke.

"He seems to have suffered some kind of brain trauma. We will have to remove him from the ship." The doctor then began to write something else on the clip board. He still had the same somewhat apathetic look on his face.

"Don't you even want to know what happened?" Lisa was furious. This man seemed as unconcerned as Devaney had been.

"Fine, what exactly happened?" Blain sounded a lot like a man who'd just had his dinner interrupted by an annoying phone call from a telemarketer.

Lisa explained while the doctor listened with a completely uninterested look on his face. Finally when she was finished, he let out an audible sigh.

"Your friend has had a stroke. There is nothing I can do in these facilities. So, all we can do is wait until he can be taken to a proper hospital in Anchorage. Now if you don't have any more questions, I have another patient to attend to." As if to illustrate this point, there was a thud from the next room. The doctor looked at Lisa for a moment more and then walked briskly out of the room.

Lisa stood there speechless for a few seconds. Maybe Devaney had helped the crewman after all. She shook her head again and then took Carl's hand.

"I'm here Carl. Just hang in there," she whispered.

Chapter 31

Gavon left Quintus to tend to Linus and returned to the cargo hold with Logan and Malcolm. When he arrived, Lynn filled him in on the details of the evening. After a quick glance at their drunken companions, they both agreed that she should go check on Carl and he would stay in the cargo hold.

Doctor Levandusky looked at her lover as if to say, "Interesting night, huh." Then she gave him a quick kiss and hurried out into the corridor. This was one of the strangest things she had ever seen. But there had to be some kind of explanation for Carl's condition.

The young professor shook her head. It must have been a stroke. A person Carl's age having something like that happen was certainly rare, but not outside the realm of possibility. But there was something in the back of her mind that was bothering her. It seemed that there was more to his condition than there appeared. Maybe the ship's doctor would be able to tell her more.

Doctor Blain gave her the creeps. But, since he was the only medical professional on the ship she would have to find out from him what was wrong with the student. Besides, Steve and Rick were going to be there, so the confrontation wouldn't be all that uncomfortable.

When Lynn arrived at the ship's clinic, she found one of the two men waiting outside. Lisa had accompanied Carl into the exam room. Steve looked at her and shook his head, but in a way that suggested he didn't know anything, not in a way that meant Carl was dead.

Lynn sighed and walked up to her student. She was about to ask if Lisa knew anything when the young woman came walking out of the clinic with tears in her eyes.

"What did he say?" The concern in the professor's voice was very evident.

"He had a stroke," Lisa couldn't hold back the tears anymore.

"Oh my god! How?" Steve asked as he embraced the crying woman.

"He doesn't know, but he said to get one of you."

Lynn nodded and put her hand on Lisa's shoulder before walking into the clinic to discuss the situation with Doctor Blain. As she entered, Rick returned, apparently he had gone to the rest room. When he saw that the young woman was crying, he tried to console her while Steve explained what had happened to him. She buried her head in his chest and sobbed making it difficult for him to hear the details of what Steve was telling him. But he understood the basics of what the other man had told him, and that was what mattered.

Lynn entered the cramped clinic and closed the door. When she was sure that the students couldn't hear her she turned to the doctor. "What do we need to do?" She asked.

"He needs to be taken to a hospital. I simply don't have the proper facilities here to treat this sort of thing." The doctor's lack of concern made Lynn want to kick him in the groin, but she maintained her composure.

"Well, we should reach Anchorage within a couple of days, can he last until then?" she asked.

The doctor rolled his eyes and sighed as if she had just asked him some incredibly stupid and irrelevant question. Then he looked at her again. "He should, besides we don't have much of a choice, it is the nearest port that has the facilities to treat anything like this."

"Can't we get the Coast Guard to air lift him off the ship? It would get him there a lot faster." Lynn glanced over at Carl, then back to the doctor.

"You'll have to check with the captain about that." The doctor seemed completely unconcerned about the young man and continued to scribble on his clip board.

Lynn had had enough. She slapped the clipboard out of his hand and looked at the surprised man. "Do you even give a shit that he might die?" There was a fire in her eyes that made the man step back before he spoke.

"I have done all I can for him. There is no reason for me to get emotionally involved," He said evenly.

"Well your bedside manner sucks." She was beginning to calm down a little. "By the way what happened to the man they were trying to help?"

Doctor Blain looked confused for a second then he spoke. "Father Devaney said he is fine, just a little sea sick."

Lynn nodded and left the room to find Gavon. There was something seriously wrong on this ship. Doctors and priests didn't act like this. She stormed into the corridor and almost ran into Steve.

"We are going to take him to the hospital in Anchorage when we dock there. But I am going to do my best to get the Coast Guard to evacuate him earlier. But I think that the captain will need convincing. So, I'm going to get Gavon to help. Tarvis is one of those old fashioned jack asses. He isn't likely to listen to a woman." She then turned and quickly walked down the corridor wondering what was going to happen to her student.

Chapter 32

When Lynn told Gavon what was going on, he immediately left to speak to the ship's captain. When he found him, Captain Tarvis was on the upper deck smoking a cigarette and looking at the ocean. Apparently he was unaffected by the icy wind whipping across his face.

"Captain, I need to talk to you."

The overweight man simply turned and looked casually at him.

"We need to get a hold of the Coast Guard, so we can air lift Carl to a hospital."

"He'll be fine. We will be in Anchorage in two days, maybe three." The captain said absently, took another drag off his cigarette, and turned back towards the waves.

"How the hell could you know that? You aren't a doctor! He could have any number of things go wrong that could kill him." Gavon yelled at the smoking man.

Captain Tarvis turned to face the angry professor. When he responded, the smell of his breath hit the Texan so hard, he actually winced and backed up. "This is my ship, and I make the decisions!"

"We are talking about someone's life here, how can you be so callous? Besides, this is one of my students, not one of your crew men. I am responsible for him."

Tarvis smiled, "We are probably out of radio contact right now anyway. He can be taken off when we reach Anchorage."

"That's not good enough! You need to at least try to contact them." Gavon was visibly angry by this point. His fists were balled at his sides and the color of his eyes went from blue to a grayish green color.

"And if I don't? Will you make me?" The captain let out a small laugh and looked at the angry man in front of him. After all what could some book worm possibly do to a man who had lived the kind of life he had.

Gavon sighed, "What are we seven years old and on a play ground here?"

Tarvis laughed a little and didn't say anything.

"If I have to," the professor continued. There was a sudden extreme calm in his voice.

The captain laughed loudly and turned away from the slimmer man. Then he spun back around and took a swing at the professor. But Dr. Stills was far too fast for him. He easily ducked under the punch. Then, from a crouch he landed his elbow squarely on the jaw of the overweight man. His cigarette went flying into the ocean and the captain fell back onto the deck of the ship.

He looked up in a daze and saw the angry professor standing over him. "Do you need anymore persuasion?" Gavon asked as he brought his boot down on the captain's hand. He didn't put all his weight on it, but just enough to let the man know that if he tried anything then he would have some broken fingers for his trouble.

The captain shook his head and laughed. "Alright, I know when I'm beaten. I'll radio the coast guard. Now help me up." His voice seemed almost jovial, but his eyes told a far different story. This man would kill the professor if he thought he could get away with it. Professor Stills knew that this was not over.

The Texan hesitated for a moment, not knowing exactly what to expect. Then he extended his hand, ready to react if the other man tried to pull him to the deck. But the captain simply got to his feet nursing his jaw with his left hand and laughed again. "It's been a while since someone was able to do that to me. Where did you learn to move like that?"

Gavon responded, "After we see to Carl, I'll think about telling you."

"Alright, let's go. But someday I want a rematch." Tarvis was almost pleasant now. This behavior was something that confused the professor more than anything else, but he shook his head and let it go. Then he followed the captain to the bridge.

The bridge of the Perseverance was set high above the deck to give a better view of what was in the distance. It was a rather spacious room with everything that could be expected in a large vessel designed to be at sea for long periods of time. There were three crewmen present. One was at the wheel and the other two were looking at the various instrument panels. All three of these men looked surprised to see Gavon entering behind the captain. It was clear that they were not used to seeing anyone but other crew members on the bridge.

Tarvis seemed to disregard all of them and walked straight to the radio. He tried on several frequencies and got only static. Then he got a response. The Juneau was a Coast Guard ice breaker in the general vicinity of the Perseverance. The captain of the other vessel got the coordinates and said that he would immediately dispatch a helicopter to evacuate the sick student.

At about 10:30 the next morning a helicopter with the clear markings of the United States Coast guard circled above the ship, and finally landed on the helipad where several people waited to help load the unconscious student. The pilot allowed two people to accompany him, one was Lisa. The other was Linus. In spite of a massive hangover, he felt that it was his duty to make sure that the student was safely transported to the hospital.

As the director was getting onto the chopper, Father Devaney began trying to convince him that he should go instead. Mitchell tried to say something, but looked like he was about to throw up instead. So Gavon intervened. "Get out of the fucking way."

The bishop looked surprised at the remark, but Logan actually chuckled at the comment. He had figured that he'd be the first of the group to tell the bishop to fuck off. So he was surprised and, in his own way, proud of his friend. The priest then tried to move past the group and get on the chopper ahead of Linus.

Lisa's eyes widened as the clergyman approached. But as he tried to push past the director, Doctor Stills grabbed his shoulder and pulled him back. Once he was standing in front of the professor, he smiled his devilish smile, and took another step towards the helicopter. This time Gavon actually put his hand on the other man's chest and pushed him hard enough to cause the bishop to stumble a little as he took a few steps back.

His eyes then settled on the professor's. "You don't have any idea what you are doing, do you?" he said evenly.

"Yes I do," Stills replied. "I am looking out for my students, not for whatever your feelings may be. If you think that it is personal, you're wrong, at least at the moment. But if you try to get on that chopper again, I will have no problem dropping you, priest or not."

"You would raise your hands against a man of God?" Devaney asked.

"I don't have time for this right now." Gavon turned to the pilot of the helicopter and gave him the signal to take off, now that everyone was on board. The pilot nodded and another crewman closed the large sliding door on the side of the helicopter.

Everyone moved back as the vehicle lifted off the deck of the ship. While they watched it rise up and then begin to fly away, Devaney tapped the Texan on the shoulder. "I think you owe me an apology, Doctor Stills."

Gavon looked at the clergyman. The fatigue was very apparent in his face. He hadn't slept all night, and still hadn't even had any coffee. "I'm only going to say this once Marco. Stay the hell out of my way, and leave my students alone." Then he turned and walked away with Lynn and Logan.

Devaney watched him go and smiled to himself. "God's judgment will find you," he yelled as they walked away. The professor started to stop, but then Lynn touched his arm and he kept walking. The bishop watched them go for a few seconds, then looked away from the group and began to walk towards the bow of the ship. If he had waited another few seconds he would have seen the only response anyone in the group had given him. Logan had simply raised his hand up as if he had been stretching. Once his hand had been behind his head he had extended his middle finger in response to the priest's comment.

Chapter 33

Two days later the ship reached Anchorage. Devaney accompanied Gavon to the hospital while Logan and Lynn supervised the delivery of some final pieces of equipment to the ship. There had been quite a debate about who would go to check on Carl and Lisa. But after immediately ruling out Logan, the group decided that Gavon should go, in spite of his contempt for the cleric.

As the pair walked to the hospital, the bishop rambled on and on about the mission of the church and their new public relations campaign. But the professor said very little and didn't even make eye contact with the cleric. He just lowered his head and watched the ground as he walked, hoping in vain that the priest might shut up. His mind was on things that were far removed from the superstitions and politics of the Catholic Church. Besides, the Texan had officially put the bishop on the list of people he never wanted to see again.

His silence didn't seem to concern Father Devaney in the slightest. He continued spewing what eventually became white noise to the young professor and didn't stop until they had reached the hospital. Finally Gavon lifted his head and saw Linus walking towards him.

Director Mitchell had a haggard look about him, but to Doctor Stills he still looked a bit happier than when he had seen him last. Apparently the hangover had passed.

"He's not getting any better, but he also isn't getting worse. They simply don't know what's wrong with him." The director sighed. "They can't find anything biologically abnormal. The CAT scan's normal, and they can't find any evidence of infection. But they think that since he's stable, he might begin to recover."

"Have you been able to reach his parents at all?" Gavon asked. His voice betrayed the deep concern he was feeling for his student.

Mitchell just shook his head. "He mentioned something about them going to Australia before we left. I guess this means I'll be staying in Anchorage until you come back."

"Are you sure? I could stay…or Logan."

Linus let out a laugh. "You are the one who put this whole thing together. And Logan is…well, he's Logan. So I'll be the one staying here until you return. You should be able to remain in radio contact until you are well past Nome, and then there is the satellite phone for emergencies."

Gavon opened his mouth, but the director answered before he could ask. "I'll call with updates on Carl's condition. I'm sure that the captain will relay them to you. Besides, I think I owe you after the other night." He then smiled a little, as if he had been talking to a friend.

The young professor looked skeptical. He had not been impressed with Tarvis, or any member of the crew for that matter. But he told himself that maybe his encounter with the captain was coloring his perceptions of everyone not from the university and let the conversation drop before it started. "What about Lisa?" Stills inquired.

"She refuses to leave him, no matter how hard I try to convince her that there is nothing that she can do. She will be staying here too, I guess."

Gavon started to ask if he should try to talk her out of her decision, but realized that it was pointless and would only add more stress to an already nearly unbearable situation. "I want to see them both before I head back to the ship. Could you take me to their room?"

"Excellent idea," the professor jumped a little, he had almost forgotten the cleric was standing there until he spoke. "I'd like to see how he's doing as well."

"Alright, let's go then," Linus turned and began to walk back inside the hospital.

"Wait, I don't think that you should come," Stills said sternly.

"You would deny a man of God access to those who are suffering?" The bishop looked shocked, but Gavon could tell that he really wasn't.

"Cram it Devaney! I know how little you actually care about Carl and I am in no mood to pretend I think otherwise. Neither Carl nor Lisa likes or trusts you. So I have no intention of letting you come with me to see them. Besides, I don't think that God has anything to do with your motives."

Linus had turned back around to face the pair and was now standing and watching the conversation with his eyes wide and mouth slightly open in surprise. During the earlier confrontation between the two, the director had been doing his best not to throw up. So this sudden outburst was something of a surprise to him. Devaney sneered and looked the young professor in the eyes. "I think that it would be a good idea to let me see them, Doctor Stills."

Gavon thought that he felt something, not unlike a falling sensation in the pit of his stomach, but then it was gone and he glared back at the clergyman. "Well, your opinion means about as much to me as a wart on a baboon's ass, and I am much more concerned about my students than you are. So you are going to have to stay away from them. Besides, don't you have something you are supposed to be doing here anyway?"

Devaney looked genuinely surprised. He hadn't expected Gavon to lash back at him. Then his eyes narrowed and he spoke in a tone that was so low that is gave the professor chills when he heard it. "Soon you will learn the error of your ways. Divine judgment will find you before long." Then the bishop turned and walked briskly away, to see to his own business in the city. The professor was very tempted to shout something vulgar at the cleric, but instead he closed his eyes to get a hold of his emotions. After a few moments he opened them and stood for a moment.

Gavon watched him go for close to a minute. Then he slowly turned to face the director, who was still standing with the same stunned expression on his face. Almost a full minute passed before either said a word or even moved. Finally, Linus spoke in a surprisingly calm voice. "I wish you would be a little more polite to our sponsors Doctor Stills. After all they are paying for this expedition."

The Texan looked the director squarely in the eyes ignoring his comment entirely, "I can't be sure why, but there is something about him, and the rest of the crew for that matter, that makes me nervous."

"Are you sure it isn't just your imagination combined with your pre-existing distrust of all things religious?" Linus asked.

"Not entirely, no. But he is hiding something, I'm sure of that. And I don't have a distrust of all things that concern religion. You are a religious man, and although we don't always agree, or even get along, I trust you."

Mitchell smiled a little, but before he could say thank you, Gavon continued.

"That's why I'm going to ask you to do something for me. While we're away, take care of Lisa and Carl. Keep that priest, or whatever he is, away from them. I'm not sure what he wants, but whatever it is, it isn't good. That man has an agenda, and he sees everyone around him as a pawn. Will you promise me you'll look after them?"

Linus could see that Gavon, who was usually so laid back, was very serious about this. He had also been talking to Lisa quite a bit in the past two days and now had developed a different view of Devaney as a result. So he slowly nodded his acceptance of Professor Stills' request.

The professor smiled a little and the two entered the small hospital. It was not the sort of huge complex that he was used to, after all M.D. Anderson in Houston was what he used as a comparison when he thought about medical facilities. So this was quite a change. But there was a pretty significant difference in the sizes of the population in his home state and this one. How many people actually lived in Alaska anyway, 50 or 60? Gavon laughed to himself. Sometimes Logan's smart assed comments made their way into his thoughts, even when he wasn't around.

The pair stopped outside the room where Carl was currently being cared for. Gavon opened the door slowly. Lisa was sitting in a chair by the unconscious man's bed, his hand was in hers and the young woman was talking to him about how she was going to show him Times Square and Central Park as soon as we was well enough to travel. After a few seconds Doctor Stills sighed and stepped into the room.

Lisa looked up and then did something unexpected. She jumped out of her seat and gave the professor a big hug. "I don't know what to do Doctor Stills. I mean I can't stand being helpless like this."

"Hang in there Lisa, he'll pull through. Just be there for him."

She sat back down and took Carl's hand again, "Thanks. I will."

Gavon relayed the messages from the other students, Lynn, and Logan. Then after an hour or so he left the two students in the care of Mitchell and walked back to the ship alone. It was almost November now and in spite of the fact that it was 2:00 in the afternoon, the stars were out already. To the north he could see the spectacular display of the Aurora Borealis. It was mostly a green glow, but he knew that other colors existed and was anxious to see how it looked north of Nome. He had begun to think of the land to the north as the land of twilight, even if the reason for the expedition had been a hoax, the professor was still glad to be able to be in The North at a time of year when few had seen it.

Gavon walked up the gangway onto the ship. He lingered for a moment and looked at Anchorage. It looked so peaceful and helped to ease the pain he was feeling for his students. No one was even walking the streets except for a lone man. The professor assumed it was a man, but the individual was bundled up so heavily that it was impossible to even tell how much he weighed. The man was walking hurriedly toward some undoubtedly warm building.

Then it dawned on him, it was bloody cold. His mind had wandered so much on the walk back that he had managed to forget the sub-zero temperature. The professor was wearing several layers of top of the line arctic gear and still was beginning to feel it. He made a mental note to wear a few more layers in the future and hurried below deck.

Stills found Logan, Lynn, and a few of the students in the cargo hold that had been virtually indistinguishable from a frat house just a few days before. But it looked quite different now. There were a few more crates, two more snow mobiles and right where he had been dancing a few nights ago there sat a huge tracked vehicle.

Gavon kissed Lynn and continued to study the vehicle. It was about twice as large as a full sized pick up truck, and of a similar shape. The cab could hold 6 people comfortably and sat towards the front of the vehicle. Behind it was a flat bed with a hydraulic lift under it. This enabled the bed to be lowered completely onto the ground to make loading easier. This could be quite useful for transporting a half ton unconscious grizzly bear.

"Heh, heh, heh, cool." Gavon said in his best Bevis impression. This brought a roar of laughter. It was good to hear them, the past few days had been so stressful there was a need for something to bring some joy into the air or at the very least take their minds off of Carl. Lynn looked at him and smiled, she understood why he had done something apparently so out of character for someone with a doctorate.

"I take it you approve of the Kodiak," She said, the smile had not left her face.

"Yes I do, I can't wait to give it a try."

"So how is Carl doing?" Her mood changed dramatically when she inquired about her student.

Gavon sighed, "The same. No better, but no worse either. Lisa's holding up pretty well."

"Poor kids, I can't believe this happened to them."

"I'm sure that they will make it through alright." Logan had been surprisingly quiet to this point. "They're both stronger than they seem."

"I hope so," Gavon replied, but in his heart he knew that they were not going to be fine. He was filled with that same sinking feeling he had gotten as a child when his grandparents had died.

"Well, I guess we should get some dinner so we can get one last look at the city before we lose sight of it. As if to emphasize this statement there was a very subtle jerk, followed by the faint humming that indicated the ship's engines were powering up. So the group proceeded to the cafeteria for a meal that was just north of fast food in terms of quality.

Chapter 34

Once the voyage was back underway, there was a much more somber tone among the students and the three remaining professors. It was clear that they were all concerned about their sick comrade. The fact that both Devaney and Mitchell were no longer on the ship brought little comfort in light of the fact that Carl was in the hospital suffering from some unknown illness, which could easily kill him. Even Logan was more subdued than usual.

The British professor had gone above deck for a bit to clear his head. He walked quietly along the edge of the ship, apparently oblivious to the wind and the cold. Even the occasional spray of water did little more than cause him to rub his eyes a little. Finally he stopped and put his gloved hands on the railing of the ship. As he stared out at the blackness of the ocean he began to think about things.

There were so many things in this world he didn't understand, in spite of his genius level intelligence. How had this all happened? Here he was an orphan from England sitting on a ship off of Alaska in the dead of winter. Logan finally had everything that he had every wanted, but never thought he could have. He had a great career, an education, respect, and most importantly friends.

Yes, friends. They were the most important thing to him. There was no question in his mind that he'd die for the few people who he called friends. But it was that very thought that was troubling him so much on this particular night. What had happened to Carl had scared him, something that was not easy to do. It was bad enough that something like that had happened to someone so young and apparently healthy. But what terrified him the most was the thought that it could have happened to someone he really cared about. If something like that had happened to Gavon or Lynn, he wasn't sure he'd be able to handle it.

On top of that, there was still something odd about the whole situation. Carl had been given a full physical before being permitted to sign up for the expedition, just like all of the students. If there had been something wrong with him, there would have been warning signs, and the doctors would have discovered it. But all of their exams and blood work had found nothing out of the ordinary. Something just wasn't adding up.

Maybe it was something that Devaney or the one of the other crew members had done. Or maybe it wasn't, the doctors had found no evidence of poisoning, so that wasn't it. But even if the clergyman had done something to the student, then the question remained as to why.

Logan knew that there were things in this world that most people were unaware of and that men in positions of power are capable much greater evil than others. Everyday seemed to further blur that line between reality and fantasy for him. Now some of the things he'd seen before he had met Gavon now came back to the forefront of his mind. He really had hoped that he could leave those things in his past. But if this was something like what he'd experienced in his younger days, then that wish would go unfulfilled.

Logan sighed. There were some things that he'd never told his closest friends. Maybe he should share some of his past with them. It was possible that some of the things he had witnessed when he was younger may prove useful, although he didn't see how at the moment. But that really didn't matter, they were his friends, and as such they should know who he was, darkness and all.

Doctor Logan Fry looked up at the stars. It was time that he let someone actually know him. Gavon and Lynn were the only family he had, so they needed to know everything, good and bad. He decided he'd tell them as soon as the opportunity presented itself.

He then yawned and stretched. It was late. But with no sun it always felt late here. Doctor Fry looked at his watch. It was 2:00 in the morning. He'd been up here thinking for hours. The Brit turned and walked back to the staircase leading to the lower decks. Even the idea of sharing his past with his friends, was oddly cathartic. He'd been keeping secrets from everyone for so long that he felt like he was going to explode. He smiled a little. Would they even believe him?

Chapter 35

After a relatively uneventful voyage, the ship reached its final destination. They had received word from Linus, and little had changed. Carl was still in a coma and the doctors still couldn't explain why. Gavon decided that it would be best to begin what they had come all this way to do. Hopefully it would help get everyone's mind off of their sick friend.

Doctor Stills took a few of students and Logan out the next day to have a look around. And under the watchful eyes of Malcolm and Quintus tried to see what they could find. It was nice to get off of the ship and onto ground that didn't move. The group carefully negotiated the broken ice pushed up by the ship and after about ten yards reached smooth unbroken ice covered in snow. Gavon, being a Texas boy, thought that it was odd how the snow actually kept the ice from being slippery.

The group walked a short distance and then out of the corner of his eye Professor Stills noticed movement. When he turned to see what had happened he saw Logan laying flat on his back. He walked to his friend as quickly as he could and was about to say something when he realized Doctor Fry had not slipped and fallen. He was actually making a snow angel.

The three students stood giggling at their teacher. Then one of them, Kumar, flopped down next to him and began doing the same. Gavon laughed a little and shook his head. He had just opened his mouth to say something to his friend when Logan kicked his legs out from under him.

He landed flat on his back and lay there for a few seconds, while the students had a good laugh. Once the laughter subsided, he let out a sigh. "Oh, what the hell," he said as he joined the others in their silliness. The entire group played in the snow for a while and enjoyed the moment. At that point in time, it felt good to be alive.

Meanwhile Lynn gathered her students in order to prepare equipment to collect ice cores from a nearby glacier. This would be a good opportunity for them to get some first hand knowledge of something that there was very little of in the California countryside. Her students would also enjoy the diversion from the monotony of classes. But part of her, the selfish part, wanted to play with some of the new toys that the university had paid for.

The students helped to unpack the crates in the cargo hold. Unfortunately not everything was packed in the proper place, so they had to go through all of them in order to find what they needed for the expedition. But, aside from making a mess, that didn't make much difference. Only one group would be allowed off of the ship at a time. Malcolm may be a lot of things, but careless is not one of them. He and Quintus made it pretty clear that they both needed to be present on any outings.

This had irritated Lynn and Gavon a little, but that was only due to their excitement over actually being somewhere other than at sea. They both knew the reasons without Quintus having to explain them to them. These two men were paid a lot to make sure that nothing happened to the professors or the students, and as a result would not be questioned in their decisions.

So, since the Texan had won the coin toss, Doctor Levandusky and her students would have to wait an extra day. But, at least it would give them time to go over some last minute details, and get used to the gear a little bit before rappelling down into an icy crevice. She looked at her watch. It was just about time for lunch. So she gathered her students and the group made its way to the cafeteria. Gavon and the others were already starting to eat. So she got her food and sat down next to him. The next day would be interesting. After all, it would be the first time anyone would be able to test-drive the Kodiak.

Chapter 36

The next morning the entire group watched as the Kodiak was lowered down onto the ice. This would be the real test as to whether Gavon had been right in is assessment, or whether the machine would become little more than a 30 ton rock on the ocean floor.

The chains supporting the huge piece of equipment became slack and the machine was now being fully supported by the ice. After a few minutes it became clear that it would hold. The ice was so thick that it had not even groaned as the enormous weight of the Kodiak was lowered onto it.

Gavon let out a sigh of relief and started to walk towards the massive machine. The ice was not as slippery as he expected, and it still amazed him that he was able to walk at a normal pace. Then he felt a hand on his shoulder. The young professor turned to see Malcolm looking back at him.

"Sorry mate, but I am paid to keep everyone safe. That includes you. So I guess I get to be the first one to take it for a spin." The Australian smiled and then walked past Doctor Stills toward the vehicle.

After taking a closer look at the ice supporting the machine The Australian looked back at the others, who were watching him some distance away, and nodded. Then he climbed into the cab and started the engine.

The Kodiak sprang to life and the group was amazed at how quietly the machine operated. Malcolm moved the machine farther away from the ship and when he was satisfied that there was no more danger of collapse, he turned off the engine and got out into the cold. Soon he was joined by the others who had followed on snow mobiles.

"Well, I hereby declare this vehicle safe," Malcolm laughed.

"You already knew that, you just wanted to drive it," Gavon replied, laughing a little as he did.

"Guilty as charged. But it worked. Didn't it?"

Lynn watched the whole spectacle from the deck of the ship. Finally as the group began to drive away into the dark wilderness she let out a sigh. Something was troubling her, but she wasn't sure what it was. She looked at her students, then at the half a dozen crewmen that had also gathered to watch the first expedition depart. Then the young professor shook her head. Why was she worried? Gavon was more than capable of taking care of himself. Besides Logan and Malcolm, crazy as they were, would never let anything happen to her love.

"Alright, show's over." She said to the group of students as she started walking towards the stairs leading below deck. The students began talking among themselves as they followed their teacher to the cargo hold. They were all eager to get started, but they would have to wait until tomorrow. In the mean time, Lynn had told them that they would be practicing their rappelling in the cargo hold, so that she could be sure that everyone would be ready for the next day's activities.

She knew that they were all competent climbers, but she had to do something to pass the time. Besides, free rappelling was something she enjoyed. It felt like what she imagined it would be like to master gravity. After all, it was essentially a free fall then, a sudden stop, but not in the painful kind of way. She hoped the students would enjoy it too.

Chapter 37

Gavon's group set out in search of their quarry. After about two hours, they decided to split into two groups in order to cover more ground. Rick was visibly happy when he found out that he would remain inside the heated cab of the Kodiak with Doctor Stills. Robert was just as excited to be able to drive one of the snow mobiles along side Logan. Malcolm decided to go with Logan and Quintus stayed with The Texan. The two groups were going to stay in the same area, but they would be searching different parts of it in order to increase their chances of finding something.

At about 3:00 pm, Gavon's radio chirped and he heard Logan's voice. "I think we see something. It's hard to tell, damn night vision goggles, but it is pretty big and actually headed this way. I think it's a bear. Either that or some fuck wit without the sense to be inside when it's this bloody cold. Kind of like us if you think about it. Why don't you guys head this way and we can do this thing? I'm freezing my balls off out here."

"Alright, we have your position," Stills replied looking at the three blinking lights on the Kodiak's GPS monitor. "We should be there in about ten minutes. If you can get a dart into it maybe we can get back to the ship and celebrate."

"That sounds good to me. It will be good to get out of the cold at least… What the hell?"

"Logan, what is it?"

"There are three more of them, no four. They are too big to be a pack of wolves. Jesus! There's another one. Oh shit!" The there was silence on the radio. In the distance Gavon, Quintus, and Rick heard the sound of gun fire. Then they heard it again, and again. Quintus looked at the professor and student. Then he sped off towards the sounds without a word, brandishing his rifle.

Doctor Stills tried to keep up, but the Kodiak was painfully slow compared to the snow mobile Quintus was riding and before long he was out of sight. By the time they reached the location, it was over. Two of the snow mobiles were wrecked, and there was blood everywhere. In the low light and greenish glow from the aurora it didn't look red at all, but more of a purplish color. But there was no doubt in Gavon or Rick's mind as to what it was.

The professor looked around. There was no one. The tracks from Quintus' snow mobile trailed off into the woods, apparently he was following something. There were also strange footprints in the snow heading in the same direction as Quintus' vehicle and they could faintly hear the hum of its engine in the distance. Stills thought for a moment. What had done this, and more importantly where was everyone?

From inside the cab of the Kodiak, his eyes surveyed the scene, while Rick sat next to him with a mortified look on his face, but he kept quiet. That was one of the things Gavon liked about this kid. He knew when to ask questions, and when to shut up. Finally the professor's gaze settled on what looked like a wide track of blood in the snow, as if someone had been dragged.

It started next to one of the wrecked snow mobiles and trailed off into the darkness. His eyes slowly followed the trail until it stopped a short distance away.

The professor's heart skipped a beat as he tried to make out a dark lump in the snow. He nudged his student and pointed. Rick nodded and aimed the vehicle's spotlight at the object. It wasn't an object at all. It was as Gavon feared, it was a body. This area had quite a few trees and the two realized that there was no way to get the large machine any closer to the person lying in the snow.

Stills reached for the door's handle, but then he thought about it. There was no telling what was out there, and if it was still around. He sighed and shook his head. "Hand me that flare gun Rick," he said softly. It was the only thing that resembled a weapon in the cab of the massive vehicle, other than the tranquilizer gun, which would work too slowly in this situation. They had given the majority of the weapons they had to the other group, since they were all on snow mobiles and didn't have the benefit of the cab of the Kodiak for safety. Rick complied and Gavon opened the door after telling him to stay in the vehicle.

The Texan took two steps and then stopped to listen. When he heard nothing, he began to slowly walk toward the motionless person on the ground. The night was eerily quiet, and every shadow in the woods seemed to hide some monster from his nightmares. But the professor continued on, his eyes darting around trying to see any possible danger.

About half way between the vehicle and the body, Gavon noticed something in the snow. It was a combat knife, like the one that Malcolm carried. He quickly realized that it wasn't similar to Malcolm's, it was the Australian's. Stills had last seen it when it had been given to Robert to hold on to. He picked it up and looked around again. There was another set of tracks going off in the same direction as a set of boot prints, and by the look of them, whoever had made them had been running…fast. But he would have to wait to follow them. Right now Stills needed to find out who the lump in the snow was, and more importantly if he was still alive. His eyes scanned the nearby groves of trees and his ears listened, but the only sound was that of the snow mobile in the distance and the snow crunching under his feet.

He cautiously approached the body. He realized that he would probably have to turn his flashlight on in order to see who it was. This was something that he did not want to do for two reasons. The first was the fact that he really didn't want to know who it was. But the second was a more practical one. If Gavon turned his light on, then his night vision would be lost for a minute or so and let anything that was nearby know exactly where he was. This would give whatever had done this plenty of time to creep up on him and do the same to him.

He reached the body and instantly knew that this man was dead. It was Robert, he could tell by the Steelers jacket the student wore, or rather what was left of it. His throat had been completely ripped out, and his torso torn open. If he had turned on his light he would have found the man's heart and bits of his lungs and liver strewn about the area. But in the low light all he could make out was the man's intestines that resembled a grotesque group of giant worms crawling out of the body. The snow in every direction for several feet was stained with his blood and gore. He couldn't help thinking how much the scene resembled a lion's kill. Gavon felt a little bit of relief that it was not Logan lying dead at his feet. But then that thought made him feel somewhat ashamed.

Before he had time to think much more about it, there was a noise as the Kodiak's door was opened. He started to yell at Rick to stay in the cab, but when he turned he saw the most frightening thing he had ever seen.

Two creatures were attacking Rick as he tried to fight them off with the stock of the tranquilizer gun. They were the size of a normal man, but covered in thick greasy hair. Both appeared to be wearing the remnants of clothing, although it was little more than rags by now. The creatures reached for the student with clawed hands that moved so quickly it was hard for Gavon to make out much in the way of detail.

The terrified young man lifted the stock of the weapon and brought it down with such force that there was a cracking sound when it connected with the face of one of the creatures. It released the grip on his leg and stumbled backwards. In the second that he was free, Rick rolled backward and out of the opposite door of the vehicle to try to find a safer position.

But as soon as he hit the snow the second creature was on him. Gavon raised the flare gun and leveled it at the stunned creature and pulled the trigger. The flare struck the creature in the side and it let out a howl of pain. This distracted the creatures long enough for Rick to scramble around the front of the vehicle. But the horrible thing that had not been stricken by the small fireball quickly followed him.

Gavon's hopes lifted a little when the hair on the creature began to ignite. But that hope was quickly dashed as he saw the first creature raise a clawed hand and bring it quickly down behind the Kodiak. There was a gurgling sound that must have been Rick's attempt to scream, then the awful sound of tearing flesh from bone as the creature disappeared from view.

It then quickly stood back up and leapt on top of the vehicle, then onto the ground about twenty feet from the professor. The other creature was still burning, and in spite of its best efforts, seemed unable to dowse the flames in the snow. Of course this was little consolation to the now defenseless professor.

The glow from the flaming creature enabled Gavon to get a better look at what he figured was his death. The claws on the creature's hands were about an inch long and slightly curved. Just how sharp they were, didn't really seem to matter to him, as the beast's arms were heavily muscled. Its black eyes glared at him as it opened its mouth to reveal large canine teeth that still had small chunks of flesh that could only have come from Rick, as they were still oozing blood. Gavon was reminded of the wolf man from the old horror movies. But there was nothing at all humorous about the way this thing looked. It was nothing less than terrifying.

The professor then glanced down at the empty flare gun, and remembered the knife in his left hand. He dropped the now useless gun and switched the blade to his more competent hand. Gavon held the weapon steadily in his right hand as the creature studied him and licked some of the residual blood from its lips. It seemed to know that he was going to be more of a challenge than the student had been.

He glanced at the blade and tried to remember what he'd been taught about fighting with a knife. But then he actually laughed at his own stupidity. "Good idea, Gav. Learn how to fight with a sword. It's such a useful skill to have. After all there are a lot of fucking swords just laying around for people to use. It was much better idea than learning how to fight with something you might actually need to use one day, you moron" he muttered to himself. Why had he never bothered to learn how to properly fight using something with a blade shorter than three feet? If he had been holding a sword, of any kind, or a staff, then he was fairly certain he would have had a chance. But the knife might as well have been a spatula for all of the good it would do him.

But then something else something far more terrifying than the possibility of his own death, entered his mind. Gavon realized that if this thing managed to kill him, then Lynn would lead a search party to find his group. As a result they would probably meet the same fate at the hands, or claws, of these creatures. The young professor knew couldn't let that happen, he had to live. His mind raced, Doctor Stills was no longer concerned with his own well being. The pangs of fear in his stomach melted away as he realized that all of the students, and more importantly Lynn, would be in extreme danger if he fell to this thing. All of the rage in his heart came to the surface and he did what the creature least expected. He charged.

The creature didn't quite know what to think of this, as the man came toward it brandishing a knife. It certainly had not expected it. But the beast stood its ground. As its eyes followed the blade and it licked its chops. Gavon drew closer and the beast prepared to tear off man's arm and as a result render the knife useless. Then it felt a little bit of confusion as the blade seemed to be moving away, drawing its gaze with it.

Before it could realize what was going on, the professor's boot struck the creature in the side of its head hard and sent it tumbling away. The creature wobbled a little, but didn't fall. It turned and put one of its clawed hands to the side of its head and rolled its eyes clearly dazed by the attack. The kick had struck the beast squarely in the ear, and apparently ruptured the ear drum. It staggered around shaking its head and trying to regain some sense of equilibrium. Then the beast let out a howl of rage and looked up just in time to see its own death in the form of the huge tracked vehicle bearing down on it.

Gavon had kicked the creature. But instead of following up with another attack, he had continued on to the Kodiak as it fell to the side. As the creature staggered around trying to figure out what happened, the professor had turned the vehicle to face it and pushed on the gas. The beast tried to leap clear of the machine, but as it turned the right track rolled onto its foot, crushing as well as pinning it. The creature fell backwards and the machine continued forward finishing the job.

From within the cab, Gavon heard the creature's struggles and cries of pain, mixed with the crunching sounds of the creatures bones being turned to powder. Finally there was a loud pop that the professor assumed was the creature's skull and it was over.

Doctor Stills turned the vehicle around to inspect his work. The creature was an unidentifiable streak of red foulness, hair, and bits of bone that had been churned into the snow as the vehicle passed over it. Then the professor realized that the first creature, the one he'd set on fire was still moving, although it looked quite different with all of its hair burned off. But Doctor Stills didn't even stop to ponder how much it looked like a man, as the tracks of his vehicle chewed the creature into a reddish brown paste.

After he'd dealt with the two creatures the Texan sat back, and made sure that the doors were both locked. He scanned the scene. Unfortunately there was no reason to check to see if Rick was alive. When he'd gotten into the vehicle, the professor had seen what was left of his student, his head had been completely severed from his body and the rest of him had been almost unidentifiable. He pounded on the steering wheel with a combination of anger and frustration and then looked up again. Finally he saw something that gave him a little more hope.

Malcolm was sitting against a tree with his rifle lying in his lap and his .45 automatic still in his right hand at his side. Two of the creatures were lying lifeless in the snow in front of him. What relieved Gavon even more was the fact that Malcolm's left arm was moving slightly, as if he was motioning for the professor to come over to him. Stills was then faced with the same difficult decision. He was certain that as soon as he got out of the vehicle more of the creatures would attack him. And he might not be as lucky this time. But he also couldn't leave his friend there to die, no matter what the risks.

The man from Texas unlocked the vehicle's doors then opened them both. If he had to make a mad dash for the safety of the cab, he didn't want to have to worry about opening them again. He jumped out with the knife in his hand and slowly walked over to his friend. His eyes continued to scan the darkness and he listened for the sounds of foot steps, but all he heard was the sound of the snow mobile in the distance, and it seemed to be coming closer. He hadn't heard any shots, so maybe Quintus had lost whatever he was chasing.

The professor shook his head, even if there had been shots fired, he had been too concerned with saving his own skin to have even noticed them. Hell, a bomb could have gone off and he might not have noticed considering what had been going on. But it was slightly comforting to know that help was on the way. So with another scan of the surrounding area, Gavon continued slowly toward Malcolm.

He looked at the two creatures as he passed. One was laying face down with the left side of its head in little pieces splattered on the nearby snow bank, like some kind of grotesque modern art painting. And the other was lying face up with its mouth open, seeming to be staring up at the flashes of green light in the sky. It had been shot through the left eye. Both were very dead.

    He knelt down in front of Malcolm and picked up the pistol. After a quick check to see if it still had rounds, which it did, he looked around again before addressing his friend. But Malcolm was the first to speak. "I always knew you were a smart one," he coughed. "I would have helped, but I can't feel my arms anymore." He had not been trying to get Gavon's attention at all. Malcolm had been trying to raise his rifle.

    The Australian was much paler than he should be, that was apparent even in the low light. Then Doctor Stills discovered why. There was a large piece of his inner thigh missing and blood was pouring out. One of the creatures had apparently bitten him and taken away a large section of his Femural Artery. He also had been slashed across the chest and his lungs were filling up with whatever blood was not spilling onto the snow. There was no doubt in either of their minds that Malcolm St. Cloud would not be leaving this place.

    "I'm sorry Malcolm," was all Gavon could manage, as the emotion of the whole ordeal had begun to take hold.

    Malcolm smiled back at him. "No worries mate. I chose to walk this road. Now I guess I've found where it leads. But it was a hell of a ride." The Australian then tried to laugh, but instead coughed up blood.

    His friend tried to say something, but the words wouldn't come. So he just lowered his head as Malcolm continued speaking his final words.

    "It's not that bad. I'm not in any pain… Do you hear them?"

    Gavon looked up, "Hear what?"

    "The bells, they line the road that leads to our destiny. I hear them now, calling me."

    Stills suddenly remembered, "Malcolm, where's Logan?"

    The dying man didn't even seem to hear the question. "Logan's not like them you know, he's our mate. Good beer too…lots of hops."

Malcolm's words were making less sense, and the professor knew he would be gone soon. But his last moments with his friend would not be peaceful ones. Gavon heard footsteps behind him. He spun around as fast as he could and saw one of the creatures begin to spring at him. His hand leveled the pistol and squeezed the trigger, but nothing happened. Snow must have melted and run into the weapon when Malcolm fired it. Then it apparently refroze and immobilized the hammer preventing the weapon from discharging. The young professor knew that he would not be able to get out of the way before the creature was on him. "Shit!" was all he managed as he closed his eyes and braced for the impact.

Chapter 38

Lance and Steve looked out into the endless twilight, entranced. It wasn't snowing, or windy, but it was still bitterly cold. And why wouldn't it be they were near the Arctic Circle after all. The other students seemed to be just as hypnotized by the harsh beauty of this place.

Dr. Stills had been right when he had referred to this place as the land of endless twilight. The combination of the moon light reflecting off of the snow and the Aurora Borealis made this place far from the black void they'd been expecting. This dazzling show is had been the reason the half dozen students had braved the cold instead of remaining below deck with the others.

Lance turned to face the group, he looked as if he was about to say something meaningful, but all that came out of his mouth was, "What the?"

The others looked at him with puzzled looks on their faces until Jaime finally turned to see what had stopped him from speaking. For a second or so the young woman wasn't sure exactly what she was looking at either. But she recoiled in horror as the impossible scene registered in her mind.

Walking toward the students was a group of creatures that resembled either werewolves or big foot depending on whether a person had watched more horror movies or Discovery Channel specials. There were four of them and their posture and movements left no doubt that they viewed the students as prey.

The other students turned to see what had frightened her, and then began to back up as she had done. Lance was the first to act, as he had realized that the group was trapped. The graduate student looked around for something to use as a weapon and found a six foot gaff lying on the deck nearby. He quickly scooped it up and told the others to get behind him. The blonde haired man couldn't believe what he was seeing, but wasn't going to waste time trying to figure it out at the moment. He held the gaff like a medieval pike man, pointing the hooked end at the approaching monstrosities.

As the creatures closed in, Steve picked up a nearby piece of wood that had been part of a crate until that morning and joined his blond friend to make a stand. The two looked at each other as if to say goodbye. But before either could utter a word, it began.

Two of the creatures charged Lance and the other two attacked dark haired man. There was a loud crack as the board in the second man's hand shattered against the skull of the first creature. It fell back and the other one pounced on him. As the creature landed on top of him it drove its claws into his stomach. Steve was knocked down against the deck as the creature rode him to the floor, ripping the life out of him as they fell.

Then as soon as Steve hit the floor, followed by the creature, it let out a wail of pain. The man had managed to drive the sharp piece of wood that remained into the creature's abdomen. A slight smile crossed his face as he breathed his last. At least he was going to take one of them with him.

Lance turned and tried to help his friend. But as soon as he did one of the creatures was on him. The hook on the gaff caught the beast that had just disemboweled Steve in the shoulder and sank in deeply. And in spite of the massive impact of the second creature, the blond man managed to keep his grip on the weapon. As he struggled with the two creatures, he was thrown back against the rail of the ship. This caused the hooked creature to screech in pain, then to try to leap towards him.

The force of the attack caused the man to lose his balance. He leaned back too far and realized that the only thing preventing him from falling overboard was the very creature that he had sunk the gaff into. He pulled at the creature, hoping that it would try to struggle away and as a result pull him back into relative safety. But, instead another creature leapt on him. It bit down on his right arm and there was a crunching sound as both bones in his forearm snapped. He released the gaff, involuntarily, and grasped the creature with his left arm.

In the next instant he realized that he was falling. Then there was a loud cracking sound and blackness. Lance had fallen overboard, taking the creature with him.

The pair fell and impacted the ice below. The student was killed instantly when his neck snapped. But the creature survived for a few seconds until they both slid down the ice into the sea. It struggled for another twenty seconds before the icy water robbed its arms and legs of the ability to function. Then the two were swallowed in icy blackness forever.

Jaime and the others began to run in all directions, much like a group of frightened rabbits. And the remaining creatures eagerly pursued them. One was slightly slower than the others, as it had a large piece of wood protruding from its mid section and a large bleeding wound in its shoulder. But this was of little comfort to the students who were now running for their lives.

Jaime looked back in time to see the creature which had a bleeding shoulder leap on one of her classmates. The young man let out a yelp and began struggling with the creature. He was a junior from Chicago named Jason. Jaime knew there was nothing she could do for him. So she ran as fast as she could, over cargo boxes and the other random items that now littered the ship's deck. Finally she spotted the ship's crane. After a quick look around she climbed into its cabin and closed the door. As she crouched in on the floor board she began to silently weep for her friends who were all surely dead.

Chapter 39

Lynn was preparing to demonstrate the proper technique for descending into an open cave by rappelling from the steel rafters of the cargo hold. Her blond pony tail swished back and forth as she checked her rock hammer to make sure that it wouldn't fall and then pulled the rope up and carefully coiled it into the bag she had fastened to her left leg. When she was sure that everything was in order, she removed the stereo's remote from her pocket and pushed pause. Metallica was just starting Fuel, with the San Francisco Symphony playing with them. As soon as the music stopped, the students turned and paid attention.

"Very good, I didn't even have to tell you. Now I guess you all know why you are on this expedition and some others aren't." She smiled. "I'm going to demonstrate how we are going to rappel into some of the ice crevices we will be visiting tomorrow. We will be free rappelling from the top of the ice caverns and trying our best not to damage things before we've had a chance to look at them. Does anyone have any questions before I begin?"

"Professor, why don't you just let the rope out all the way and just rappel as normal?" Gerald asked.

"Well, we are going into crevices that have never before been seen, and I don't want the rope to damage the walls or contaminate our samples. But more importantly if we are rappelling down to get someone who's fallen, it would be better if the rope didn't slap that person in the face. One very important thing I want you all to remember. Be sure to tie a knot in your rope a couple of feet from the end, so you don't just slide right off the end of it."

This seemed to make sense to the students and Gerald nodded. The rope wouldn't cause nearly as much damage as a person, but since that aspect could be minimized and the other couldn't, it made sense to keep the rope contained. The professor asked if there were any more questions, and when no one spoke, she prepared to descend to the floor.

Then there was a strange sound in the hallway, like someone walking with a clicking sound after each step. Kumar looked at his professor, and when she nodded, he casually went to the door and peered into the hall way. He expected to see a crewman or one of the two remaining monks, but instead he saw a baffling, as well as terrifying sight.

The creature was coming down the corridor sniffing the air and swinging its head from side to side to try to pick up the freshest scent. The Indian ducked his head back inside before it could see him and motioned for everyone to be quiet and to hide.

Lynn thought about saying something, but when she saw the look of sheer terror on the student's face, she figured it would be best to stay quiet and find out what was going on. The other five students realized that something was very wrong, and when Kumar ducked behind a stack of crates, the others followed suit.

The room was completely quiet. The only sounds were the scraping of the ice on the ship's hull as it rose and fell a few millimeters with the water below, and the sound of those strange footsteps. Kumar was cursing himself out in his mind for not closing and locking the door, but that couldn't be helped now. The footsteps were getting closer and he figured the creature was probably at the door by now. The Indian wanted to try to peek out and see if it was coming in or not, but reason won out over curiosity and he stayed hidden.

Lynn, on the other hand, had a perfect view from her perch in the steel beams of the ceiling. She felt herself gasp silently as the thing entered the room still sniffing the air. It put one clawed hand against the wall and looked around the room. The professor could clearly see the blood dripping from its mouth and wasn't surprised when the hand left a bloody print as the creature moved away. It was wearing what used to be clothing, but now more resembled shredded bits of cloth stained with copious amounts of gore.

The hair around the creature's mouth was wet and matted with fresh blood and small pieces of flesh from whoever had been unfortunate enough to encounter it last. Lynn became concerned for the students who were in the dorms and the cafeteria. There was nowhere to go for them and this thing had pretty clearly killed recently. But the young professor tried to put those thoughts out of her mind, there was nothing she could do for the others. Doctor Levandusky assumed she was safe, being twenty feet from the floor, but her students were all hiding where the beast was sure to find them given enough time.

The creature slowly walked into the room and began to look around. It licked some more of the fresh blood from its mouth and opened its mouth into something that resembled a demonic smile. Then its eyes fixated on a stack of crates, behind which Stephanie and Gerald were hiding. They hadn't made any sound that Lynn had heard, but the monster was apparently convinced that there were people hiding there. It began to move purposefully toward the hiding place.

Lynn's mind raced, if she yelled, then everyone would probably come out and start running. The creature was sure to catch at least one or two of them. If she did nothing, then Gerald and Stephanie were as good as dead. The young woman had to act quickly, but how?

Then it came to her, it was a long shot, but as Gavon would say, sometimes the only way to win is to risk everything. As soon as the creature was directly beneath her, she pushed play on the stereo remote. The creature spun around with surprising quickness to face what it perceived to be a threat, as James Hetfield's voice blared from the speakers.

Lynn took a deep breath and put the rest of her plan into action. With her rock hammer in one hand she gave the rope some slack and began what was essentially a free fall. As soon as she was in range, she swung the hammer down as hard as she could.

The combination of her downward momentum and swinging at the same time provided enough force for the woman to drive the pointed end of the tool deep into the creature's head. As soon as she connected there was a cracking sound as the point penetrated the creature's skull. The force caused her hand to release the handle, but this was something she had expected. Her other hand instinctively pulled the rope behind her back and she came to a stop behind the creature, just half a foot above the floor. For a split second, she was glad that she had used a static rope to rappel with. Dynamic ropes were a lot like giant rubber bands. They prevented a person from having a sudden jerk when stopping. But in this case it would have stretched causing her to slam into the floor, rather than stop.

Lynn put her feet down, stood up, and took a couple of steps back, away from the creature. The satisfaction she felt quickly turned to fear as the creature didn't fall, but slowly began to turn and face her. Her brilliant mind couldn't understand how the creature was still moving with four inches of steel lodged in its brain. The professor took another step back and tried to free herself from the rope, but her hands were shaking badly from the impact and excitement, and she kept fumbling with the carabiner's locking gate on her harness. The young woman realized that she would have to look down in order to release herself, but she couldn't take her eyes off of the hideous thing that was turning towards her. She could try to simply pull the rope through her figure eight, but the safety knot at the end of the rope would not be able to pass through.

Just as she managed to loosen the gate lock enough to unhook from the rope, the creature crumpled to the floor and began to twitch. It let out a large breath, but didn't make any other movements. The handle of the hammer moved slightly in time with the creature's slowing pulse. Apparently it had contacted a major artery in the creature's brain. Finally it was still as the creature's heart ceased to beat, although its limbs continued to twitch sporadically.

After about thirty seconds her shaking hands were able to finally free the young woman from the rope. By now several of the students were peeking out from their hiding places to see what was happening. Lynn looked around and then quickly back at the creature on the floor. She cautiously walked over and kicked it hard in the ribs, then jumped back out of its reach. But the creature remained motionless. She seemed satisfied that it was not going to rise again and walked back over to the lifeless thing, her eyes never leaving its still form.

The professor bent down and took a hold of the handle of her hammer. She gave it a slight tug, but it refused to budge. As Lynn pulled the creatures head moved with the hammer. The young woman sighed and then put her foot on the creature's head and gave the handle a quick jerk. As the point of it came free of the beast's gray matter there was a sucking sound not unlike when a boot is pulled from a mud puddle. Then it was free. As soon as the hammer was out, the creature's head rolled slightly and blood, bits of brain, and skull began to ooze from the large hole. After a few seconds the puddle under its head ceased growing. Lynn then was sure that the creature was dead, since it indicated the heart was no longer beating. She stood in stunned contemplation for a moment or so. Then she realized that this may not be the only one of these things. The young professor motioned for the student who was closest to the door to close it.

Her name was Dana Mathers. She was a plain looking senior with brown shoulder length hair, who's been accepted to Texas A and M for her master's work. She would have gone on to a very successful career in the oil industry. But instead her life was cut short as one of the creatures in the corridor pulled her through the doorway and tore her to pieces. She managed the beginning of a scream, but that was all before the beast tore her throat out.

The second creature stepped into the room while the first remained in the hallway and finished ripping the life out of the young woman. The remaining students tried to duck behind whatever cover they could find. But the creature seemed fixated on Lynn, who was in the middle of the room. It had the same devilish smile that the other one had had. As the creature began to charge she held her hammer ready in a vain attempt to defend herself, and thought of Gavon.

Chapter 40

Doctor Stills braced for the impact of the creature. The Texan was going to try to fall backward with the beast and attempt to use its own momentum to throw it free of him. From there he wasn't quite sure what he was going to do, but he was certain it was going to painful. For now all The Young professor could do was wait to react. It seemed like an eternity, but in a situation like this one time seems to slow down. Every second becomes a century, or at least long enough for a man to think about all of the things that he should have done differently in life. Gavon had always wanted to take Lynn back to the Amazon with him. Maybe even get married there.

But the impact never came. As the creature pounced, a dark figure slammed into its side and rode it to the ground. The creature and the dark figure began to roll in the snow like two wrestlers, but with much more blood and hair splashed around. The bewildered man watched wondering what exactly was going on. Then his confusion peaked, the dark figure was another of the creatures. Its hair was slightly darker that the other, but it was definitely one of them and it looked pretty pissed off.

Doctor Stills wasn't sure what he should do. It was pretty clear that this new creature was attacking the other. But the professor had no idea what it would do if it managed to kill the other, or at least drive it off. For all he knew, he was going to be dessert.

The two creatures broke apart and stood facing each other. They both had received bites and scratches, but those on the original creature were far worse than those of the newcomer. It had a deep gash in its stomach, just below the ribs and its right arm hung lifelessly at its side. When the creature moved it became apparent that there were at least two extra joints in its arm above the elbow. The first creature glared at the newcomer and growled. It was a low, almost inaudible sound that seemed to be punctuated by what must have been a cough. It was hurt pretty badly.

Gavon then realized that the blood around the creature's mouth did not come from some unfortunate person who'd become prey, but was coming from the creature itself. It was pretty likely that the new creature had managed to puncture at least one of its lungs. This brought a slight smile to his face. The thought of one of these things suffering a little seemed like a bit of justice to him. He began to consider how to slip away into the darkness, but there was nowhere to go. Both creatures were blocking his path to the Kodiak. Most other people would have started running anyway, but the professor was much smarter than that. If he stayed here at least he could see the creatures, and maybe take advantage if one creature got the better of the other. So he stood watching the two creatures and waited for whatever was going to come.

The newcomer stood looking at its opponent as if studying it. Even in the dim light Gavon could see that its eyes were darting from point to point on the injured creature trying to assess where would be the best place to strike. Then its gaze met the others and they stood motionless, snarling at each other. Each seemed to be waiting for the other to make the next move.

Finally the new creature leapt forward, bringing one clawed hand directly into the creature's uninjured arm and the other into its throat.

There was a brief struggle and then the sound of tearing flesh as the newcomer tore the other's trachea completely free from its neck and then unceremoniously tossed it into the snow. Then the dark creature sprang backwards away from the dying one. It stood and watched the beast's final death throws with almost casual interest.

The monster grabbed the place in its neck where its trachea had been and took a step toward the newcomer. Then it fell to its knees, all the while making a sickening gurgling sound. Gavon couldn't help but feel a little bit of pity for the creature, in spite of the fact that it had just tried to kill him. But that went away quickly when he thought of the two dead students and Malcolm. The creature then fell forward, and began to open and close its mouth, reminding the professor of a dying fish. He then realized that the new creature was watching him intently.

Stills slowly turned to face the creature while the other breathed its last breaths. But he was surprised to see that the creature was not preparing to leap on him and rend him to pieces. Instead it sat on the nearby wreckage of a snow mobile and picked up a jacket in one hand while trying to brush the snow off of it with the other. Gavon immediately recognized the jacket as Logan's.

Once the beast seemed satisfied that the jacket was as clean as it was going to be, it turned back to face Gavon. There was an eerie feeling in the pit of his stomach as he faced the creature and slowly pulled the knife out of his belt, where it had been since he had picked up Malcolm's pistol. Then it started quickly towards him with surprising speed.

Doctor Stills held the knife up, ready to strike. But the creature simply batted it out of his hand and moved past him to where Malcolm lay. The now very confused professor turned to face the creature and witnessed yet another odd behavior. The great hairy thing knelt down and gently reached out to touch Malcolm's face, but then pulled it away when the man's skin proved cold to the touch. The beast sat back, looked toward the sky, and howled. It sounded oddly human. Then the creature turned to face Gavon, who was surprised again to see tears in its eyes. Just as he started to speak, Stills heard the distinct sound of a clip being slammed into an assault rifle.

"Gavon get down!" Quintus yelled as he leveled his weapon at the creature.

But the young professor did the opposite. He stood up and turned to face his friend. "Wait, don't shoot!" He shouted back as he approached a very confused Quintus.

Stills reached the other man and put his hand on the weapon. He then pushed it slowly away from the creature. Quintus' eyes were wide and fixed on the thing that his friend was apparently trying to save. "What in the hell are you doing!"

"Returning a favor, besides you know that creature."

"Have you been hit in the head? Get out of the way before more of them show up." He was apparently calming down a little, analyzing the situation. But the adventurer was more than a little confused as to why this creature was sitting in the snow and not attacking. Then he realized the creature was actually weeping. He then looked at Gavon with a puzzled look on his face.

"I think that it's Logan," he said quietly. "He saved my life, and didn't get upset until he saw what had happened to Malcolm." The mention of his dead friend's name seemed to bring to the surface all of the emotions he had been forced to suppress for the last half hour. He'd been so focused on trying to stay alive that the professor hadn't even heard Quintus, as he pulled up on his snow mobile, or the shots that the southerner had fired, sending another creature into oblivion. But now things were beginning to register in his mind. Two of his students were dead. One of his friends was dead, and another was apparently a werewolf. He lowered his head and tried to stop the tears, but strong as he was, the Texan found that he was powerless to do so. His legs began to grow weak and he had to sit down.

Even Quintus Vale, who normally had a face of stone, shed a tear for their departed companions. But he never took his eyes from the creature kneeling in the snow beside Malcolm's body. Then the adventurer witnessed something spectacular. The creature's hair began to fall out and its features became more human. Its large canines seemed to retract into its mouth and became normal teeth. The claws on its hands retracted into its fingers and it began to cough. Vale realized that Gavon had been right. He was now looking at Logan Fry.

The Englishman knelt in the snow shirtless and weeping over the body of his friend. The sub-zero temperatures didn't seem to have any sort of effect on the man. In fact there was steam rising from his bare skin and the snow around him had begun to melt.

After a few moments he stood up and quietly whispered, "Goodbye mate." Then he turned and began to put on the sweater and jacket that were lying on the vehicle behind him. They didn't fit nearly as snugly as they once did on account of the fact that the layers he hadn't managed to strip off before his transformation were now merely random strips of fabric strewn about the ground. The little bit that he still wore was hanging in tatters from his neck by what was once the collar of his thermal undershirt like some sort of tribal necklace. Fortunately his pants had survived the ordeal for the most part and although they were far from new looking, they were at least still serviceable. Somehow his boots had also managed to stay intact, except for the large holes where his claws had extended.

Doctor Fry began to walk towards his two remaining companions, but he stopped beside one of the dead creatures, reached down, and picked something out of the snow beside the lifeless corpse.

"What is going on Logan," Gavon managed to ask in a weak voice without turning to face him.

"I'll explain later, but we need to get back to the ship right now," he said in a surprisingly even voice.

"I don't think there are any more of them around, other than you of course." Quintus' voice was strong and determined. He still held his rifle, but didn't seem to want to use it on Logan at the moment. "We need to see to our friends, we can't just leave them here."

"We are going to have to." The Englishman's voice betrayed a sense of urgency. "We need to try to save the ones who are still alive!" He then opened his hand to show his friends what he had found in the snow.

It was a small golden cross with a round, red garnet right where Jesus usually hung, on a twisted golden chain. Quintus and Gavon knew immediately where they had seen one exactly like it in the recent past. Every member of the crew seemed to wear one. Stills leapt to his feet, drawing on every bit of will power he had. This new determination pushed aside the sadness that had almost completely overtaken him and gave him a new feeling of strength. He was not going to lose anyone else who was dear to him, at least not today.

The professor pushed past Fry, hurried to where Malcolm's body lay, and rifled through his coat to find three extra clips for the pistol he now carried and a box of cartridges for the rifle that lay in the snow. He scooped up the weapon and started to jump on the Englishman's snow mobile, which was the only one that still functioned, other that the one Quintus was riding. Then Gavon felt a hand on his shoulder. It was Logan.

"You need to thaw those out or they aren't going to fire." The Brit's voice was calm, as if he knew that it was the best way to get his friend to pay attention.

Doctor Fry was right. The ice inside the pistol was not going to thaw if he was riding a snow mobile at full speed in sub-zero temperatures. As much as he didn't like it, he was going to have to have to take the Kodiak. It was significantly slower, but he needed the heater in the cab in order to make his weapons useful again. He nodded and the two sprinted towards the large tracked vehicle. Once inside he started it up and in his haste almost left his friend standing in the snow. But Logan managed to dive into the cab before the vehicle really began to move.

Gavon didn't even turn to look at his friend or apologize. But that didn't bother the Englishman. He understood that his friend was entirely focused on one thing…Lynn.

Chapter 41

Jaime poked her head out from inside the cab of the crane. The entire deck was covered in blood and gore. This caused her to vomit as her gaze settled on what looked to be someone's arm that had been gnawed to the bone.

Her eyes scanned the deck and she noticed that there were many more bodies than there were people who had accompanied her to the upper deck. This could only mean one thing. Whatever those things were, they had gone into the dorms too, everyone was dead.

The young woman vomited again at the thought of all of her friends having met such a gruesome end. She tried to identify some of the bodies, but was unable to at first. Then her gaze settled on a group of three. One of them was Samantha, who'd been taking a nap in the girls' dorm. Another was Brad. He'd been in the cafeteria with the majority of the other students. The third body was unidentifiable and she quickly looked away. Jaime was certainly going to have nightmares about this for the rest of her life, which she realized might be relatively short if she didn't get back into her hiding place.

She quietly closed the door to the cab and curled up into a ball. The young woman remained like that for quite a while, silently weeping. After what seemed like an eternity she heard something that sounded like a string of muffled gunshots. Then a metal door slamming shut quite some distance away. Then there was only the wind.

After several more hours, she heard the sound of a large motor steadily moving something very heavy. She realized that the main door to one of the cargo bays was slowly being opened. It was the same one that had been opened in Anchorage so the crane could lower the Kodiak into the cargo hold. Her hopes were lifted a little bit, since the doors moving meant that someone was still alive. But she had to know who.

The young woman carefully looked through the crane's wind shield and saw smoke coming from inside the hold. Then she saw someone trying to climb out from inside the smoking room. It was Kumar. But he couldn't seem to find anything to hold onto. The Indian cast a terrified glance back into the hold and then tried to scramble out. But then he lost his grip and disappeared from view.

The next thing the young woman saw made her heart skip a beat. One of the creatures sprang from the hold and pulled itself onto the deck of the ship. As soon as it was on the deck it looked around. To her horror, its fiery green eyes settled on her for a moment and Jaime knew that she was looking at her death. The student ducked back out of view, hoping that the creature hadn't seen her. But she knew that was as unrealistic as children thinking that hiding under a blanket would keep them safe. She curled up and waited for the inevitable.

Chapter 42

Lynn's eyes widened as the creature began to close rapidly. It came at her bent at the waist, but with its head up and clawed hands out in front like some horrific line-backer. She realized that it intended to tackle her then finish her once she was on the ground.

The beast closed until it was near enough to make a final lunge. But the nimble young woman quickly dropped to the ground and rolled to the side. Unfortunately, she wasn't quite fast enough and a couple of claws tore through her left pant leg, leaving two gashes on her thigh. They weren't very deep but they still hurt when she sprang back to her feet. The young woman didn't waste any time worrying about that though. The creature came to a stop and turned to face its intended prey. Lynn spun around to face the creature and realized that now her back was facing the door, and more importantly the second creature in the corridor.

The beast snarled at the woman and studied her for a moment. It apparently was surprised that the professor had been so nimble and was now trying to figure out how to best trap its prey. Either that or it was waiting for the second creature to attack her from behind. Lynn stood trying to listen for the second creature, while trying to keep an eye on the one in front of her. The faint sounds of chewing and tearing flesh told her that the creature in the hallway was still preoccupied. The sounds made her shutter a little, but she was still glad that it wouldn't be grabbing her from behind just yet.

The creature's muscles tensed as it prepared to charge again. But then something hit it in the head and shattered when as hit the floor. Lynn quickly realized that it had been a beer bottle. The creature turned just in time to see Gerald standing on top of a crate and catch a second bottle in the face. The creature roared in anger and began to charge the student, but as soon as he jumped back behind a stack of crates it whirled around and once again came straight at the professor. The young woman held her hammer and waited. This time when she moved to the side she planned to try to strike at the creature.

But she didn't have to. There was a loud crack from behind her and a small hole appeared in the right part of its forehead. It slowed and straightened up, but continued to advance. Then a second shot rang out and a larger hole appeared where the creature's right eye had been. The remains of its eye ran down its face like the yolk of a freshly cracked egg and fell to the floor leaving the optic nerve hanging out of the freshly made cavity. Three more shots rang out before Lynn saw Gavon step in between her and the creature, holding what looked like a .45 automatic.

She had never seen anything shot before, and was slightly surprised that it was not anything like the way it was portrayed in Hollywood. The creature's head didn't explode in a graphic display of gore and it didn't fly back with the drama of an old western.

The creature simply stopped and then fell forward. But her lover didn't stop shooting. As the creature lay on the floor he proceeded to empty the clip into what was once the back of the creature's skull, but what remained now resembled bloody hamburger meat with bits of bone sticking out of it. Doctor Stills stood and continued to pull the trigger in spite of the clicking sound each time that indicated the weapon was empty.

Finally she lightly touched his arm and after pulling the trigger two more times he turned to face her. His eyes looked strange. They were not the color of the sea that they normally were. Instead they seemed to almost glow with a green fire and his face had the twisted expression of a mad man. Lynn realized that she had never seen Gavon lose his composure before. It was actually quite frightening. The professor's eyes were no longer those of a scientist, looking objectively at the world. They were those of a cold blooded killer.

Then his features seemed to soften and he collapsed into her arms. They held each other for what seemed like a life time. Each was so incredibly relieved that the other was more or less alright. After a few moments they broke their embrace enough to look each other in the eyes. They were both crying.

She stared to speak, but his kiss stopped her. It felt so good to be in his arms again. He held her and her fear melted away. In spite of all the carnage and horror that surrounded them, she felt safe. Even the gashes on her leg didn't hurt anymore. Finally the young woman looked up and saw Quintus kneeling down over the remains of the other creature.

Then she saw Logan look over his shoulder down the hallway and shove the southerner into the room. He then quickly followed and slammed the door behind him. The two then began to turn the heavy wheel that locked the door.

As soon as door was secured, the adventurer looked around for a moment and then picked up one of Lynn's extra ropes while the Englishman continued to hold the wheel of the door. He seemed to be struggling to keep it still.

"I don't mean to be a bother, but I could use a little help here." Logan yelled as he strained to keep the wheel from moving. The creatures on the other side of the door were apparently trying to turn it from the other side.

The two lovers released each other and ran to the door to help their friend hold the wheel steady while Quintus weaved the rope around it and then around the metal bracing of the wall. After he was satisfied that it would hold, he did the same to the other side and then stepped back to inspect his work. The others slowly released the wheel and when it barely twitched from the creature's efforts the all breathed a collective sigh of relief.

Lynn then turned to Logan and gave him a hug. He returned the favor and then looked around the room at the assembled students. There were so few of them. His expression changed from relief to sadness.

"Are there any others?" He asked in a shaky voice.

Lynn simply shook her head, in spite of the fact that Fry already knew the answer to his question. She then turned to Gavon and started to ask about Malcolm and the two students, but he just looked at the floor and shook his head.

"What about the others, the ones in the dorms and the cafeteria?" she asked quietly.

Doctor Stills was unable to answer, so it was Quintus who finally spoke. "I'm sorry," was all he needed to say. The group had passed by both dorms and the cafeteria on the way to the hold and had encountered horrific scenes in all three places, particularly the cafeteria. Most of the students had been relaxing and drinking coffee together when the creatures fell upon them. There was nowhere for any of them to go. The result was an unimaginable slaughter. A few had managed to make it up onto the deck, but had encountered the group that had attacked Lance and the others, which meant they had only lived a few minutes longer than their friends who had died in the cafeteria.

The survivors sat in silence for a long while, letting the reality of their situation sink in. Everyone seemed to be stunned by what was happening. All except Quintus who used this time to clean his weapons and reload. The adventurer seemed to be filled with purpose, rather than sadness. And it seemed that he knew more than he was telling them. Finally Gavon looked at the southerner and asked, "Quintus, what the hell is going on?"

"I'm not sure that you would believe me if I told you." He responded almost casually.

"We have been fighting werewolves that have killed most of my students and one of my good friends. I have to say that I will believe just about anything at this point." Gavon said in a tone resembling something close to normal. But he was still not quite calm.

"I don't even know where to begin." Quintus said calmly as he slammed a fresh clip into his sidearm.

"How about just what in the hell these things are. I think that would be a good place to start," the professor said angrily.

"Well, should I tell them? Or do you think you'd be more knowledgeable Doctor Fry?" He said as he cast a lazy glance at the Englishman.

Lynn looked slightly confused when she spoke. "Logan?"

He looked at Gavon who let out a sigh and nodded.

"Well, first of all, they aren't exactly werewolves. But they might be the source of that myth," Professor Fry began as the others cast confused glances in his direction.

Chapter 43

Logan Fry sat cross legged on the floor of the cargo hold sipping a beer that he had gotten from the nearby refrigerator, as the others gathered around him to listen to his tale. To an outsider, this scene may have looked like it belonged more at a children's camp than on a ship beset by strange beasts near the Arctic Circle. The Englishman was surprisingly calm as he began the story of his life, and more importantly how he came to be what he now was.

He had grown up with his mother, at least for his early years, and had never known his father. This could have been for any number of reasons, but since his mother had never told him much one way or another about the man, Logan had surprisingly little ill will towards him. Without a steady father figure, the young boy was forced to learn about being a man from whoever he could. Most of these surrogates were found in the pub where his mother worked.

As a result of this unconventional upbringing he had been forced to grow up fast. The boy had learned how to settle disputes with bullies with the oldest form of communication, his fists. His only escape from the hellish world he lived in had been in books, Logan had developed a hunger for knowledge early in life, and that had stayed with him as he aged. Of course this bookishness was the very thing that had made him a target of larger and less intelligent children on the playground. After a while he had proven himself, and the bullies began to bother him less and less.

One day he had come home from school to find a strange man waiting for him outside the door. This was not really all that unusual, and he had learned to accept this sort of thing as part of the tavern worker's life style. But the lad soon realized that the man was with the police. It didn't take long for him to figure out that something had happened, something bad. Then the man confirmed to him that there had been an accident and his mother was dead.

Logan paused for a moment as the thought of that dreadful day so long ago seemed to revive the memories and feelings he had repressed for so long. His eyes moistened a little, and he coughed once. But after a moment he took a drink, composed himself, and continued.

"They took me to the station and called someone to get me. Everything was a blur and finally I was being led away by a man who I later found out was a priest. He took me to an orphanage where I stayed until I was sixteen. That's when I liberated myself from those bastards, along with a substantial sum of the church's money. But after what I'd been through in the four years I was there, I figure it was only a small percentage of what they owed me." Logan paused and took another drink from his beer before continuing.

"Why's that?" Gerald asked.

"I'll get to that, but let me continue."

Gerald nodded and glanced at the door again, it seemed to be holding, at least for now.

Logan set his beer down and continued. "At first, well once I began to accept the fact that my mum was really gone, I figured that someone would adopt me and I would have to start learning how to deal with something like a normal family. But, of course, I was too old for anyone to want to adopt me. I mean why get a twelve year old, who more than likely has issues, when you could get a baby that can't remember shit about its past? So after a couple of months I began to accept the fact that I was going to have to grow up under the care of the church. I knew that I wouldn't like it, but I reckoned that I could learn to deal with it.

At first things were about what I expected them to be. I was fed, clothed and schooled, if you want to call it that. The Bible was the major focus of all the classes. Not anything important. But I managed to get my hands on other, more useful, books as well. One day I managed to get a hold of The Origin of Species and began reading it at night. But one of the priests caught me and took it away from me. And if that wasn't bad enough, I was sent to see the Bishop who presided over the whole school.

He seemed like a relatively nice person, for a priest, and we began to talk. He tried to convince me that there was no such thing as evolution. And that I should put my faith in the lord to find the truth. But when I asked a few simple questions about how to explain certain things if the idea of evolution was wrong, he never could give me a satisfactory answer, he would just dodge the question. Finally I was up front with him and told him that his teachings made no sense to me and I didn't think he even understood why he believed the things he did. This brought about a change in his demeanor.

I was taken to a separate area, where they kept the so-called trouble makers. There were about a dozen other children in there, all of whom I'd never seen before. We were completely separated from the others, unable to interact with them or even communicate the fact that we were alive. But, I think that is how they wanted it. My guess is that they told the others that we'd either been adopted or that we'd died. Sometimes I think that it would have been better if we had, died that is.

We were kept in a small building outside of the main orphanage complex. This whole area was surrounded by high walls made of stone. I felt like a prisoner. And in reality, that's exactly what I was."

"That's horrible." Lynn gasped.

"Yes it was, but the worst was yet to come. We were denied books, toys, and anything that we did not directly need to survive. The only thing that we could do was to stare at the stars, or try to learn from each other, or fight. But unfortunately the other kids in this place with me did not have the passion for learning that I did. So I continued my education in the finer arts of street fighting. The guards seemed to delight in making us hurt each other. I think that they even bet on the outcome, kind of like betting on a boxing match. But the man in charge was the worst of the lot.

The overseer of this prison was a huge, evil man by the name of Gregory. He made us run and do all manner of exercises until we passed out from exhaustion. I didn't know it at the time, but they were preparing us for something. Finally the day came when I guess they felt that we were strong enough, and one by one we were led away.

They led me to a dark, candle lit room. Then I was hit over the head. When I woke up I was strapped to what I assume was a stone alter, but I can't be sure, with a dozen or so people standing around me in a circle. They were all wearing red robes and pointed hoods. They looked a lot like the KKK does come to think of it.

Every one of them began to chant something in a language I didn't understand, but looking back on it, it was probably ancient Greek. Finally one of them grabbed my head and another forced my mouth open. A third of those bastards poured something that tasted so vile into my mouth that I can still taste it. But before I could spit it out one of them held my mouth and nose closed. I only had two options, swallow or drown. So I swallowed.

As soon as it hit my stomach I passed out again. When I awakened, I was back in the small room that I was kept in. My stomach was aching and I felt like the pain would kill me, and I guess part of me was destroyed." He paused for a moment before continuing. "I can't remember much except that for the next few weeks we were all really sick, and a few of the other kids actually died. But then those of us who remained began to feel different. Our senses were much sharper, as well as our reflexes. I could hear things miles away that I never could before. So for the first time in a long while I was able to learn new things, simply by listening. New smells wafted into my nostrils, I could tell people apart by smell alone. I could even see in the dark as if the sun were out. At that point I thought that these new abilities were wonderful. Then we learned of the price. This was not a gift, but a curse.

Those of us who remained were taken to another place, far from the orphanage. It was another enclosure with high walls, but there was little inside other than the dirt on the floor and a few bones. We didn't know what was going on. Then Gregory yelled at us from the top of the wall. He had two other men about his size with him. And they were holding a smaller man, who looked terrified. Each of the large men was holding what looked like a gun in the hand that wasn't restraining the smaller man.

They unceremoniously shoved the smaller man into the enclosure with us and told us to kill him. At first none of us moved. We still had no idea what was going on. But then they started shooting us. It turned out that the guns they had were pellet guns, filled with rock salt. Each time one of them hit it stung and then continued to burn for a long while. At first this scared all of us and we tried to run to the far side of the pen, but there were more guards on the walls there, who did the same thing. Finally our fear began to turn to anger, which is exactly what they wanted.

I'm not sure who it happened to first, but the anger caused us to change. We became those creatures out there." He gestured towards the door. As if to emphasize that statement, one of the creatures hit the door so hard it shook. Logan shook his head and continued.

"It was a strange feeling. My entire focus was to kill, but I left the others alone. I guess it is some sort of pack mentality. But we all turned on the man that they had thrown into the pen and ripped him to pieces." Logan stopped and looked at the floor for a moment before continuing. He was clearly ashamed of what he had done.

"Part of me could see what I was doing and tried to stop the rest of me, but that conscious part of my mind was unable to do anything but watch. Needless to say it was over pretty quickly. And after a while we all got so tired we went to sleep, or passed out, which ever. When we woke up, we were human again, but we were still covered in that poor man's blood. Some of the others were excited even more about their new abilities. A few even suggested that we turn this new power against the very ones who gave it to us. But we were all just kids, and didn't really know what else might lay in store for us.

The next day the bishop himself came to see us. He seemed unafraid as he entered our prison. We quickly understood why when he held out a small device that looked like a small flashlight and ordered us to sit down. When only a few of us complied, he put it to his lips and blew. We were all struck with immobilizing pain. Then after a second or so he stopped and told us again to sit down. This time we all did as we were told." Fry paused and took another drink.

"Was it like a dog whistle or something?" Stephanie asked.

"No, it was some kind of mechanical device. They had put a small chip in the back of our necks that acted like a receiver. Hurt like hell when I dug it out after I escaped. But I didn't find it until later.

He explained to us that we were now in the service of the church, and that we really didn't have any choice in the matter. That asshole kept referring to us as the Hounds of God. But I think that Hounds of Hell would have been more appropriate. We were to be used to punish those who had offended the church, or so we were told.

What they really used us for was to terrify simple people back into the fold, so to speak. We were used to terrorize areas, mostly of third world countries, where attendance at mass was on the decline. They'd release a couple of us every night for a week or two into a small village, meanwhile the local priest would call for prayers to deal with the beasts of the night. Finally when enough people were attending mass, and tithing, the attacks would abruptly stop and the church would get the credit.

Then we'd be shipped off to some other area to do the church's dirty work. Finally one day we were taken to a small town in eastern Pennsylvania, a small town by the name of Honesdale. They'd managed to get us into the states with no problems at all, and that was when I had an idea.

In order to get through customs we'd shown our identification and I realized that somehow they'd managed to get dual citizenship papers for me, probably the others as well, but I wasn't concerned about them. They all had taken to this new "work" like fish to water. As a result I didn't consider any of them to be my friends. So one night when we were supposed to be sleeping, I waited until one of our handlers took two of my comrades out for the evening's activities and crept out of my room.

There was one guard outside of our rooms. Apparently the other two were downstairs. As soon as he saw me his hand was on his device, or whistle, or whatever you want to call it. But I acted like I was sick and finally he came over to me. As soon as I had the opportunity I swatted the device out of his had and then hit him in the chin with the strongest upper cut I could manage, but I was being very careful not to allow myself to become angry. Fortunately he went down pretty hard and was out cold. I rifled through his pockets and found the keys to one of the vans and his wallet. Then just when I was about to go downstairs I thought of something. I wasn't going to get very far without some form of currency other than the guard's credit cards. The guards had picked up a large amount of cash, shortly after we arrived in the States. My guess is it was so our movements would be harder to follow. I picked up the whistle and put it in my jacket, then went to the room that Gregory was staying in.

I knew that he would not be there since he was always the one who supervised the night hunts as he liked to call them. Just as I was about to kick the door in, it occurred to me the amount of noise it would make. So

I did something that I learned from one of the more seedy influences of my early life. I took one of the guard's credit cards and used it to open the door. We were staying in an older hotel, so the locks on the doors were pretty simple.

Inside the room I found what I was looking for, a suitcase full of cash. It didn't look like the ones you see in the movies. You know the ones where the bills all fit perfectly into the suitcase and there is no unused space. This was much more disorganized, but I really didn't care. I grabbed it and climbed out the window and down to the parking lot.

I found the van easily enough and drove off without looking back. I knew that they wouldn't be able to follow for quite a while, after all the other van was with Gregory more than two hours from our hotel. So I drove south."

"Wait a minute, why didn't they call the police?" Kumar asked with a nervous glance at the door.

"What would they tell them? That one of their werewolves stole a van and a bunch of money. No, they have their own ways of dealing with runaways. But I'll get to that." Logan sighed and took another swig of beer before continuing.

"I finally made it far enough to feel safe, so I dumped the van in Bristol Virginia and took a bus to Knoxville. From there I went to California where I was able to enroll in high school and finish my basic education. Finally I was accepted to Cornell and well, you know the rest."

"No we don't!" Lynn was standing looking at him with her arms crossed. Her fear was gone and now she was mad. "You haven't told us anything about why you seem to be able to control yourself when you change and, more importantly, any suggestions on our current predicament."

Logan nodded and continued. "Well I learned that there is a chemical compound that can help the mind overcome the curse of the transformation." He grinned and held up his beer.

"You've got to be fucking kidding me." Gavon said quietly.

"No, I'm not," Logan responded. "The answer was in the form of this magical elixir. That is the reason I became a biochemist. I wanted to figure out what in beer was helping control the curse."

"Did you figure it out?" Lynn asked. She was apparently calming down.

"Yes, I did. It is the hops. More specifically it is the Alpha Acids in the hops that help control the urge to kill when the transformation occurs. That is why I drink so much and brew my own beer. I have to be sure that there is always enough of the chemical in my system to help me in case I transform."

"But can you transform whenever you want to?" Gavon asked.

"Yes, but it is a little more complicated. The transformation takes a lot of energy. By my calculations, it is something like 30 to 40 thousand calories. And while in that form our metabolism runs much faster. In addition to the boost of energy supplied by this increase in metabolism, our adrenal glands are constantly working while we are in that form. That's what gives us the extra strength"

"So, we could just wait them out and they will starve?" Gerald asked.

"Under different circumstances yes, but I don't know if you noticed how overweight the crew is. They've been planning this for a while. They also probably have secret food stores somewhere. Not to mention the fact that they have control of the kitchen. But it was a good idea. No, we need to think of something. Does anyone have any suggestions?"

Chapter 44

Gavon walked over to the corpse of the creature he had killed and gave it a good hard kick. Everyone watched him without saying a word, with the exception of Logan.

"Not to worry mate, it's dead," Logan stated rather matter-of-factly and then took another bite from a Power Bar.

"I know that, but I want to show everyone something." As they all gathered around he turned the body over so that the creature was facing up. Its mouth hung open so that the size of its teeth was very apparent and its remaining eye had rolled back in its head. In its chest there were four gunshot wounds, any of which should have hit a vital organ or two.

No one had even bothered to count the number of shots he had fired. And why would they, in a situation where a person's life is in danger the number of shots being fired is not nearly as important as the fact that they are being fired. No one even bothered to notice the four shots that penetrated the creature's chest, no one except Gavon that is, since he was the one who fired them. After his first four shots did not even slow the creature down, he had take aim at the creature's head. Fortunately for Lynn this had worked.

He pushed the tip of his knife into one of the wounds, and wasn't surprised when it stopped after less than a quarter of an inch. He pulled the knife back slowly and shook his head. "I was afraid of that. The ribs stopped the bullets from going deep enough to cause real damage. They must be significantly harder and wider than in any animal I have ever seen."

He turned to look at Vale who was now finished cleaning his guns and was watching the door. "Quintus, how did Malcolm know to shoot them in the head?"

The adventurer looked over at him and then at the rest of the group. Then he let out a sigh. "It's a long story."

"Well, we aren't going anywhere anytime soon," Lynn replied.

The southerner then took another deep breath and let it go. "Alright, but this is going to change your perspective on the world a bit."

"Oh please, please don't tell us anything shocking today," Gavon said sarcastically, "I don't know if we could handle anything out of the ordinary."

Quintus let out a single low laugh and shook his head. "Point taken, as you have seen these creatures are not what you would call normal. But they have strengths and weaknesses just like anything else. The best way to kill them is to shoot them in the head with a high velocity round. The skull is a little weaker than the ribs, and there isn't the same amount of give as in the chest. But it still takes a hell of a big gun to do it. Why do you think that our side arms are .45's?"

"We know that already!" Gavon was past the point of being irritated. He had realized that if this man had known the crew was full of these things and simply kept his mouth shut, then a lot of people had died for no reason.

"Let him talk honey," Lynn's voice seemed to soothe him a little bit.

"First of all I know what you are thinking and the answer is no. I did not know that the crew consisted of Diatritha."

"Diatritha?" Lynn and Gavon repeated in unison.

"Yes, that is the name given to these wolf-men by the Philistines. They were the first to encounter them, at least as far as we know."

"What do you mean by "we"?" Lynn asked as she but her hand over her lover's mouth to prevent another outburst.

"As you can see there are things in this world that should not exist, at least not in the world that most people view as reality. But we know differently. I am part of an organization that has its roots in the Bronze Age. In essence we try to prevent catastrophic events from destroying human kind. The ironic thing is that most of these threats are the direct result of people meddling in things that they are not ready for yet. In this case the Catholic Church got a hold of some ancient scrolls and translated them, sometime in the early middle ages. I wish I could tell you when, but we honestly don't know.

These scrolls were an old ritual from the time of the Philistines. Essentially they were the instructions for creating these creatures and others. Do you remember the story of David and Goliath? It was based on truth. Goliath was created in a similar manner to the Diatritha, but he was something different.

Anyway, once the scrolls were translated they were deemed to be heretical and should have been destroyed. But someone high-up in the church saw the potential and the documents were archived instead. That should have been the end of it, but it wasn't. They used the rituals to create the first Diatritha to walk the earth in more than a millennium. This is where the legends of werewolves in Europe began.

The problem was they didn't know how to control the creatures. So they would simply let them loose to terrorize the countryside. Then they would dispatch actual monster hunters to kill them. And of course the church got credit for destroying the menace and as a result increased its influence.

At some point a group of these hunters saw what was going on and broke from the church. These men were angered at being lied to, but more importantly at the fact that so many people were dying to further the pope's agenda. They were known as The Wolves of Twilight. This is the same order that Malcolm belonged to and I still belong to. But, tough as they were, that small order wouldn't have gotten far without help, especially with an enemy like the Catholic Church hunting them.

There was another organization founded in the Bronze Age. Its original name has been lost, but translated and passed down through the generations it means The Road of the Bells. The followers are known as Bell Ringers. Their purpose is to watch and guide mankind in an attempt to prevent humans from destroying themselves and the world as a whole."

"Bullshit," Was the only thing that Logan could say.

"Why? Think about how many times throughout history that mankind has been on the brink of destruction. There was the Decline of the Roman Empire, The Black Plague, and the Cold War, just to name a few. Don't you think that at least one of those, or one of countless others should have plunged mankind into another dark age and maybe even destroyed the species all together?'"

Everyone was silent, not even Logan had anything to say to that.

"The Bell Ringers saw the potential of the small order and took in the Wolves. Together the group began to systematically find and destroy the Diatritha. But they never could get them all, and then in The Renaissance the appearance of these wolf-men declined dramatically. It probably had something to do with society as a whole beginning to reject superstitions and embracing reason. As a result, the Bell Ringers and Wolves began to put their talents towards other things.

But then, about fifteen or twenty years ago they began to appear again. But this time it was even more of a problem."

"Why would it be more of a problem now that society is more advanced?" Gavon asked he was calming down a little bit.

"The very fact that society is more advanced, means that people don't believe in things like werewolves and vampires anymore. Seriously, if I had come up to you a week ago and said that there were werewolves running around and they were going to kill people, you'd have put me in an insane asylum. But now, I'm fairly certain that you see things a little differently. Wouldn't you?"

Everyone remained silent. So Quintus continued.

"This created the perfect opportunity for the church to use these creatures again. This time it was different though. They have apparently found a way to control them instead of just releasing them in an area and then killing them. As Logan mentioned there are devices they are using to control these beasts. What this means is they no longer have to destroy their creations. So, in addition to being more economical, now these creatures can grow, learn, and become something even more dangerous."

"What does that mean?" Gerald asked with a nervous look at the door. "These things already seem to be pretty damn dangerous to me."

Quintus sighed. "I know what you mean. But there are legends of creatures far greater than these. They are able to control themselves when they change, and some are even able to control people's minds. Some say they can even absorb a person's very life force with their gaze. I've even heard stories of some of them being hundreds of years old, but I don't know how much truth there is to that."

"Carl..." Lynn said softly.

Gavon looked at her then at Quintus. "Devaney? That means that Linus and Lisa are in as much danger as we are."

"It is possible, but I can't be sure. But whether he is or not, the bishop is not our most immediate concern. If we do get out of this, I will see to him. Of course any of you may come along if you wish. But I think that he will be far more dangerous than the beasts we are dealing with here, even with help. By the way does anyone know how many of them there are?"

"37 by my count," Lynn stated rather matter-of-factly. It was clear that she was still thinking about Carl and Lisa.

"How did you figure that out?" Logan asked.

"I noticed that there were far more crewmen on this ship than there should be. So I counted them. There isn't much to do on such a long voyage remember." She looked up and tried to smile but her eyes betrayed how she felt.

"Fair enough," Lynn's attention to details never ceased to amaze Logan or Gavon for that matter.

"So how many have we gotten?" Quintus began counting them on his fingers to keep track. "I got the one I was chasing, Gavon got two, Malcolm got two before… Logan got one there and one in the hallway, plus these two. That makes nine confirmed, the others may have gotten one or two, but it is best to assume that they didn't. So there are 26 plus the two monks, I think they are the ones pulling the strings in this. Damn, that's a lot isn't it?" Quintus looked around the room, "I don't suppose any of you has a mini gun do you?"

Stills looked at him and let out an irritated sigh.

"Sorry, do we have any guns here? The weapon's locker is pretty far away. I can't see how we could get to it with all of those things out there."

"Well, we've got your rifle, pistol and knife, the same from what Malcolm had, and Logan's rifle. Other than that just some rock hammers, which Lynn has proven to be effective." Gavon looked at her, the relief that she was alright was still apparent in his haggard face.

"Anything else?" Quintus asked.

"Just some crow bars and things like that, nothing that would be all that useful to us." Lynn responded.

"Well the way I see it we have no choice but to fight these things, weapons or no." Quintus stated.

"Are you insane?" Gerald's surprised voice was surprisingly loud.

"Well, that is up for debate I suppose. But what else can we do?"

"We could get the hell off of this ship and try to get to Nome." Gerald replied.

"We'd never make it." Quintus said evenly.

"We could get to the snow mobiles and the Kodiak and make a run for it." Kumar's voice was nearly as panic-stricken as Gerald's.

"No, unfortunately Quintus is right. Even if we could make it to the vehicles, and out run these things, we don't have enough fuel to make it anywhere close to anything resembling civilization. We'd end up freezing to death. I guess we have to make a stand somewhere. And this hold seems to be as good a place as any." Gavon looked at the group. They were not fighters. They were a bunch of scared kids for the most part. He knew that he could count on Lynn, Logan, and Quintus. But whether the others would be of any use didn't seem too likely.

The young professor couldn't blame them really. These were people who had spent most of their time in the class room, reading books, or in the lab. People like he and Logan were something of an anomaly in the academic world. Doctor Stills was grateful for the somewhat crazy life he had led since meeting his British friend. He walked over to his friend and slapped him on the back. "Well old friend, I guess this is going to make one hell of a story for the pub."

"Don't you mean if we make it through this thing while still breathing?" Logan asked, for the first time since he'd known him, the Brit sounded unsure of himself.

"We will. I'm sure of it." Gavon lied. In reality he thought that their chances of survival were about as good as a box of donuts at a police convention. But he couldn't let the others know that. However small their chances, they were much smaller if everyone simply gave up hope.

Stills looked around the room at the various supplies. There wasn't much to work with, but he had to think of something. Then he felt Lynn's hand on his shoulder. He turned to look at her, and was surprised to see an odd little smile on her face.

"I have and idea," she said.

Chapter 45

Gavon strained as he and the others hoisted the heavy crate into the air. Once it was suspended over the door and tied off, he wiped the sweat from his brow and stood back to admire their work. He let out a little laugh under his breath that no one heard, except Logan of course.

"I'll bet you're thinking the same thing I am." Logan then picked up his beer and took a drink.

"What would that be?"

"I feel kind of like Wiley Coyote. But I'm pretty sure that the roadrunner isn't going to be what comes through that door."

Gavon laughed out loud this time. This plan did seem to be rather cartoonish on its face, but if it worked they would be in pretty good shape. And for some reason he actually thought that it would. Then he noticed that the others were all staring at them.

"I take it everything is ready?" Lynn said from the top of the stack of crates. She and the remaining students were rigging themselves in to the support struts of the ceiling. Quintus had begun climbing the crates to join them.

"Are you sure that you want to do this? I mean I can do it if you want." Gavon said to Logan.

"Cheers mate, but I'll be fine. Besides I can't let my best mate try something that only a lunatic would attempt, especially since there is a perfectly good nutter right here. So I guess you'd better join the others." The two then shook hands and then the Englishman gave the Texan a hug, which he returned.

"Be safe," was all Gavon could manage.

"Gav, in case I don't make it…"

"You will make it." His friend cut in. "You will."

"Thanks, you and Lynn are the only family I have. Keep her safe."

"I will, but in case you need a little more motivation, when we get out of this I'm going to tell my sister know how you saved all of our asses. So you'd better be around to take advantage of being a hero. I'll even let you keep your giggle berries."

Logan smiled. "You'd better get going. This is going to happen fast. So make sure everything is ready before I open this door."

"Alright, let's do it. I'll see you after."

"Okay."

With that Gavon quickly scaled the stack of crates and joined the others. He then nodded to Logan, as he took the bulky device that operated the large door in the ceiling in his hand. Doctor Stills hoped that this would work, but more than that he hoped that he, Lynn, and Logan would be able to sit and talk about this adventure over a beer later. Somehow he doubted that the outcome would be that happy though.

The Englishman looked back and nodded, it was about to begin. Doctor Fry turned to the door and balled his fists. Then he dropped to his knees and put his fists to the sides of his head. This part always hurt. His canines extended, which felt like a bad trip to the dentist. But they soon stopped moving and he looked over his shoulder at his friends. His fiery eyes showed even brighter than they usually did.

The hair all over his body began to grow and his nails began to extend. When they did, they began to dig into the palms of his hands. He suppressed a scream of pain and rage. It was important that the creatures on the other side of the door didn't have any idea what was going on in the hold. The more they were surprised, the better.

He felt the blood pounding in his head as his heart rate increased. Then it was over. The crazy professor stood up as one of the horrifying monsters he hated so much. He had made the transformation again. Now he was ready. With a quick look at the others, he smiled the smile of a mad man and reached for the door.

Chapter 46

It happened quickly, just as they had planned. Logan cut the ropes and turned the wheel on the door slightly. But as soon as he felt the creatures on the other side grab a hold and start ferociously turning it to open the door, he let go and jumped back. The door burst open and they began to pour through.

The first two through the door were cut down by bullets through the brain from Quintus and Gavon. But this did not even slow the flood of monsters coming through the door.

Fry leapt on top of the first crate and felt the claws of the nearest creature dig deep into his leg. But then there was a report from a rifle, he assumed Gavon's, and it was gone. The Brit climbed up higher, and then managed a quick look over his shoulder at the creatures swarming after him. He wasn't sure he would make it, but so far things seemed to be going as planned.

As soon as the flow of creatures stopped coming through the door, Lynn cut the rope that was suspending the crate over the door and with a crash, it fell, blocking the exit. Gerald then threw a flaming bottle of fuel that set the crate, and more importantly the fuel canisters inside it, ablaze. Now there was little chance of the creatures getting out that way.

Doctor Fry reached the top of the stack of crates and Gerald dropped another flaming bottle behind him. At the same time, Gavon opened the ceiling giving them a way out. There was another loud crack as Quintus fired and the creature nearest Logan fell to the floor.

As soon as the door was open, people began to try to scramble out. Kumar was the first to reach the top, but he lost his grip and fell back. Fortunately he was still roped in and didn't fall to what was certain death. Then Logan looked up and sprang to the surface. His clawed hands dug into the deck and he hoisted himself out of the hold.

He looked around, and was pleased that there were no Diatritha anywhere to be seen. He was even more pleased when his gaze fell one the scared woman hiding inside the cab of the crane. Of course, he also hoped that the sight of him in this condition hadn't caused her heart to stop.

He reached down for the fallen student and unceremoniously tossed him onto the deck. Then, once Kumar had freed himself from his rope, Logan gestured toward the crane. But the Indian just looked back at him with a mixture of confusion and terror on his face. So as soon as the student stood up, Logan gave him a swift kick in the ass. This seemed to get the point across and the young man ran towards the crane.

Kumar opened the door to a screaming Jaime. He put his hand one her arm, which was defensively over her eyes and was rewarded with a kick to his jaw. The Indian fell back and yelled her name.

She opened her eyes and was surprised to see her friend trying to stand back up. The terrified, and somewhat confused, young woman then looked out at the scene unfolding in front of her. The creature on the deck was actually helping pull people out of the hold. She made out Quintus' form through the thick smoke just as he raised his rifle and took another shot into the hold.

There was a loud noise as one of the cans of fuel in the hold exploded, then another, and another. The stack of crates Logan had been standing on finally collapsed, leaving the surviving creatures trapped in the inferno.

Gavon smiled and put down his weapon in order to pull Gerald up onto the deck, while Quintus scanned the area for any other dangers.

Surprisingly, they had all made it out alive. And other than a few scrapes, bruises, and relatively minor burns they were all uninjured.

The southerner looked down into the hold and leveled his rifle at a creature looking up at him with a murderous gaze, but he didn't fire. Gavon put his hand on the adventurer's shoulder. "Let the fuckers burn." He said as the sound of their pain stricken cries pierced the night. Quintus nodded, smiled ever so slightly, and shouldered his weapon.

It wouldn't take long for the creatures to burn to death in the enclosed metal room. As the others watched the spectacle in the hold, Kumar led Jaime over to the group while nursing his jaw. Logan then looked at the group and collapsed. As he reverted back to human form it was apparent that his breathing was pretty ragged. The change had taken a lot out of him, and he was probably going to be unconscious for a few days. But Gavon had a feeling his friend would survive. He was, after all, too crazy to go into a coma and then die.

Lynn looked at her lover, "Is it over?"

As if to answer her there was another explosion from the hold and then no more cries of pain. But Quintus spoke up. "I doubt it. We haven't accounted for all of them yet. Most importantly I don't know what has become of the two monks. We need to find them then get back to Anchorage to deal with Devaney."

"And save our friends," Lynn said.

"If they are alive, that is." Quintus pointed out.

"Well, for now let's operate on the assumption that they are, shall we." Gavon said as he put his arm around his love.

The adventurer only nodded and looked toward the ship's bridge. He then sighed and began reloading his rifle. There was still a lot of work to do, but for now he would let them have their victory. These untrained people had performed far better than he could have imagined they would have. He reflected on that fact for a moment, and then looked over at Doctor Stills, who was still holding Lynn and watching Logan. "Where did you learn to shoot like that if you don't mind me asking?" He was amazed that a lab rat like Stills seemed to have absolutely no problem firing a weapon. What was even more amazing was the fact that the professor seemed to hit exactly what he was aiming at every time. In fact, Quintus was pretty sure that the professor was one of the best shooters he had ever seen.

Gavon looked back at him and smiled a little. "I am a product of the public school system in Texas. We were required to be proficient in small arms by the fifth grade."

The group looked at him and was silent. Then he heard Lynn laugh a little and he held her closer.

Chapter 47

Brother Jonathan looked out over the deck from his vantage point on the ship's bridge. How had this happened? They had planned things so perfectly. But the smoke coming from the cargo hold was proof enough that something was wrong. Then his spirits rose as he saw one of the Diatritha leap out of the cargo hold. It must be over. The loss of a few of the creatures would be unfortunate, but those that remained should be many times stronger now. This would please his masters. Perhaps now they would allow him to choose where he would go, instead of being sent to some god-forsaken wilderness again.

However his satisfaction was quickly replaced by confusion when the creature actually pulled that little Hindu kid from the hold and then began to help the others out. What the hell was going on? That adventurer, what was his name? Quintus Vale, yes that was it, was now on the deck. He took aim and fired down into the hold while the creature, his creature, helped the other scientists and students up and out of danger.

Then it occurred to Jonathan. This was the runaway. Devaney had told him that once there had been a Diatritha who had escaped in America and was never found. They had all assumed that since there were no reports of strange killings, other than those that they were responsible for, that someone had found and destroyed him. They had figured it was those damned Wolves of Twilight, since none of their own hunters took credit. But here in front of him was proof that the creature still lived. Even more strangely it did not behave like the others. As opposed to their blind, murderous rage, this creature was fully in control of itself. How could it become that powerful without feeding? Most of them had to kill at least 30 or 40 people to gain that kind of control. The runaway had only killed 6 or 7 by the time he had escaped. He must have figured out how to control himself some other way. But that didn't seem to matter at the moment.

Why had he been so ambitious? If he hadn't destroyed the satellite phone like he had been told to do, then he could call Devaney now and tell him what was happening. Stupid, the idea had been to disable any means of communication so their prey could not call for help. But now it seemed that the plan had backfired. The intended cattle were now the hunters.

The new creatures were not smart enough to have done anything except charge mindlessly into the cargo hold, which had apparently been a trap. Now they were all either dead or soon to be and there was nothing that Jonathan or the other three survivors could do about it. Just as the monk began to wonder if they would come for him and his companions next, he saw Quintus look at the ship's bridge and casually begin to load his rifle. The pudgy cleric could have sworn that the man actually smiled a little as he looked toward the bridge.

There was little time, but at least the rogue Diatritha seemed to be out of action. He probably didn't have the energy reserves to change and function with his increased metabolism for very long. It would be a while before he was conscious again. At least that was something and they still had captain Tarvis. But it was of little comfort, since the group was now making its way to the bridge and probably expecting trouble. Several of the students seemed to be carrying the unconscious Dr. Fry, wrapped in his jacket, and four of them at least had guns.

Jonathan wished that he was as powerful as Devaney. His master would be able to control the minds of these puny mortals and put an end to this. But that had not been the plan. The Diatritha had needed to feed in order to become stronger. But now it seemed that the tables were turned and there were few options left.

"What do we do now?" Tarvis sneered at Jonathan. The animalistic instincts in the captain made him understand that he was now trapped.

"What do you think we do? We have to fight."

"Do you think that you can stop any of them with that mind control shit that Devaney taught you?"

"I don't know, but I'll try."

"You'd better, because if you can't we are all dead." The captain growled.

"What about you? Why don't you do what you were created for?"

"I was created to hunt, not to fight armed people who know about us and are prepared." Tarvis bared his teeth at the monk.

"Stop it, both of you!" Samuel yelled at the bickering pair. "Don't you see, we have to think of something or we are going to be dead very soon!"

"Fine, do what you need to. I can take care of myself." Tarvis glared at the two monks. He thought about tearing the pair to pieces himself. After all it had been their incompetence that had put him in this situation.

Just then there was a sound at the door, they were on the other side.

Chapter 48

Gavon, Quintus, and the others moved together toward the ship's bridge. Whether the two monks and the captain were still there was somewhat irrelevant. If they could get to the satellite phone, the Bell Ringer could call some of his associates to go to Anchorage and try to save Linus, Lisa, and Carl. Then they could finish getting things under control on the ship.

They moved slowly, the adventurer and Doctor Stills in the front with the only rifles than had ammunition left, and Lynn and Gerald in the rear with the two side arms. The shotgun Quintus had been carrying was lying on the deck of the ship next to its empty shell casings. The remaining students were in the middle, two were carrying Logan and the others were each armed with some form of hand held item that could be used as a weapon if needed.

Finally they reached the large steel door of the ship's bridge. Quintus looked at Gavon and nodded. Lynn moved up to the front to help the southerner cover Stills as he tried to open the door. Gerald turned his back to the group to make sure that nothing could creep up behind them. The young woman and the adventurer raised their weapons and the Texan tried to turn the wheel. But after a few tries, it became clear that it wasn't going to budge.

"Well, I guess that answers my first question. I guess the monks and the captain have decided to lock themselves inside. Now what?"

Quintus looked at him and shrugged, then looked to Lynn. "Any ideas, after how well your last plan worked, I am inclined to let you figure this one out as well."

"I don't know yet, but if anything comes to me, I'll let you know. It might be possible to go in through the windows in the front. But whoever went in first probably wouldn't last long."

"Do you think that there is anything to rig onto on top of this thing?" Gavon asked.

"I don't know, but it gives me an idea."

"Is it as crazy as the last one?" Her lover smiled.

"No, it's pretty simple actually."

Doctor Stills leaned over to listen to her plan. But then he began to feel strange. Lynn's voice became distant and unintelligible. His control of his limbs was suddenly gone and to his horror he found that his arms were involuntarily moving his weapon in the young woman's direction. Worse, she didn't seem to notice.

Something was in him telling his body what to do, while his mind was still able to see everything, but unwilling to stop it. At first he thought of what Logan had told him earlier. But Gavon knew he was not like his friend. The professor realized that it must be one of the monks. Whoever was in his head was going to use him to kill Lynn and then probably the others, but he seemed powerless to stop it.

It felt like he was sleeping, somehow in the world of dreams. Everything seemed to move more slowly and the lines between the real and the unreal were becoming even more blurred. He knew he had to do something fast. As his mind raced, he remembered what his Aikido master had told him. "When you try to fight force with force, you will always fail. You must use an attacker's force against him. That way he harms himself instead of you."

He knew what he had to do. He stopped resisting the force moving his arms toward Lynn. Instead he began to try to make them do the exact same thing. The weapon moved quickly towards his love and the others realized what was happening. To his relief Lynn quickly ducked and the momentum of his motion caused the rifle and his right arm to slam into the metal wall of the hall way. The force controlling him tightened his grip on the weapon, but Gavon tightened it even more. The impact with the wall combined with the tightness of his muscles caused the weapon to fall harmlessly from his hands.

Quintus seemed to realize what was going on and quickly kicked it away. Then he told everyone to get back, which they did. The professor thought about how grateful he was that the adventurer was so alert, he would need to buy him a beer or two when this was over. Now the professor could focus on the invader. Stills dropped to his knees and closed his eyes. He let himself fall into the dream world where he felt his attacker could be found.

His dreams manifested themselves in different ways, but the one he found himself in looked very similar to the real world. He was in an open field with rocks and tufts of brown grass scattered about. The sun seemed to be in a perpetual stage of eclipse and the wind was blowing strongly enough to affect his hearing. The young man looked around for the intruder. Somewhere nearby had to be the thing controlling his body.

Gavon scanned the landscape for a few moments and soon spotted something that he knew was out of place. There appeared to be a man in a brown robe apparently wrestling with a huge snake, it looked a lot like an anaconda sized version of a Timber rattlesnake, which was an animal he had always been fascinated with. A shaman friend of his had once told him that the Timber rattlesnake was his spirit animal. The professor somehow knew that the reptile was part of him, the part that controlled his motor functions and the man was the intruder.

He charged forward and hit the man in the back with his best side kick.

The man, still entwined with the serpent tumbled away. He then tried to grab the creature once more, but the snake grew and transformed into a massive oak tree with a single large catlike eye in the center of the trunk. The brown robed man fell backwards again. But he immediately stood back up and turned to face the professor. He was smiling in a sinister sort of way. "Hello Gavon," he said as he pulled a large gleaming sword made of a strange white metal from inside his robe. It looked a lot like a Scottish Claymore.

It was Brother Jonathan. This fact didn't really surprise Doctor Stills, but the sight of the weapon did cause him to step back a little bit. The monk stood looking at the professor and smiled. "I was hoping to finish some of your friends before I dealt with you, but it seems that you are more difficult than I had expected. No matter, it's time to finish this." The monk then charged and slashed at Gavon.

The professor managed to get out of the way and moved farther out of range to avoid the next slice of the massive blade. He tried to think, "I need a weapon, but where can I find one here?" The monk charged, but the Texan was able to avoid the blow again. Although, he realized that he was not going to be able to keep it up forever. At some point the blade was going to hit him, and that would probably be the end of it. He could run and hide. But if he did, the monk would surely take control of his functions again. The young man couldn't allow that. There had to be a way to fight back.

The blade swiped dangerously close to his head and he jumped back a few more feet. He frantically looked around and saw a building in the distance. There might be something inside that he could use. Gavon was then faced with a hard decision. If he left the monk alone, then he would certainly try, and probably succeed, to take over the professor's body. This would put everyone who was with him in extreme danger. But if he didn't find a way to fight back, the monk would kill him, and probably take control of his body anyway.

Doctor Stills turned and began running toward the building, and to his relief, if it could be called that, the monk was following him still swinging the giant blade. The Texan ran as fast as he could until he reached the building. This was one that he recognized, from his nightmares.

It was an old church, much like a gothic cathedral in Europe. There were priests and villagers standing around what looked like a short telephone pole with wood and straw piled up at the base. He'd been burned at the stake enough times in his nightmares to realize what was going on. The people seemed to be waiting for him. And when they saw the professor there was a shout and the entire mob came charging towards him. He turned to try to flee from them, but in front of him stood the monk, still holding his weapon. Jonathan smiled at Gavon, "There is no where to go, it's either the sword or the stake. I'll let you decide."

Just then the villagers grabbed him, as they had so many times before and began dragging him to his fate. He tried to fight, but like every other time there were just too many of them. Dozens of hands held him, while two or three people tied him to the upright log. Then one of the priests leaned down with a torch and lit the fire. "Burn the heretic! Burn the heretic!" The crowd shouted gleefully.

This was usually the part of the dream where he woke up in a cold sweat, but somehow Gavon knew that if he died this time it would be for real. He looked at the crowd. They were the same faces that were there every time. The only difference was that this time there was one extra person in the crowd, still smiling, but now he was leaning on the sword as if it were a cane.

The professor began to feel the heat from the flames creeping closer to his feet. They had done a good job, the tinder was very dry. This meant there was very little smoke to make him pass out before the flames could do their work. He looked out at the chanting mob and the grinning monk and sighed. Being burned was something that had always haunted his dreams.

Then it occurred to him. This whole place was a construct of his mind, except the monk of course. He was the one in control of the wind, the light, the terrain, even the fire. Here he was a god. This new realization brought a smile to his face.

There was a flash of lightning and several of the people in the crowd were instantly incinerated by a bolt from the sky. Then it began to rain, dowsing the fire at his feet. The rest of the crowd began to run in all directions. But Gavon ignored them. He managed to slip his hands free and then quickly freed his feet. He then jumped down to the ground.

He stood up and faced the monk, this time the young man was the one smiling. Jonathan was beginning to charge, but stopped when he saw the expression on his intended prey's face. "What are you smiling about? Are you that happy to die?"

The gleeful man didn't answer. But as soon as the monk began to advance again vines with large thorns sprang from the earth beneath him and wrapped around his feet. He fell to the ground with a very confused look on his face. Doctor Stills stepped closer and looked at Jonathan. "You didn't think this through did you? Don't you know where you are?"

"What are you talking about?" The monk tried to swing his weapon at the chiding man, but another vine appeared and plucked the sword from his grasp and gave it to Gavon.

"You invaded my mind. That means that I am the one in control here. Any nightmares you could bring with you pale in comparison to what I can summon from the dark depths of my mind. So I say this to you, welcome to my nightmares."

The vines then tossed the confused and now scared monk a short distance away. He stood up with a bewildered look on his face and began to run. Doctor Stills simply followed him until he saw what the monk was running for. There was a large reinforced door, similar to the ones that would be found in an old castle. But this one was wide open and hanging in the air a few inches from the ground. "That must be the gateway to his mind," Gavon thought.

Jonathan was only a few steps from the door. If he could make it he would be safe. But it was not to be. More vines erupted from the ground and bound him so tightly he could not move. Then he saw the professor walk over and peer through the door. "I wonder what it's like in that twisted mind of yours Jonathan. I'll bet it's far different from what I might find if you were sane."

"Why don't you go through and find out?" The bleeding monk spat.

"I'm sure you'd like that, considering the predicament you are in right now. And I must admit I am more than a little curious. But I think we are both going to be disappointed." The Texan then grasped the door's handle and began to close it.

Jonathan screamed, "NNNNOOOOO!"

Gavon stopped, "Ah, I see that I was right. If I close this, you die don't you?"

The monk only stared back at him helplessly. If that door was closed, his body would die. It would continue to breathe for a while, but he would be dead just the same. After all it could not survive without his mind.

"But what will happen to this part of you, the one that is trapped here?"

Jonathan had never really thought about it. What would become of him if his body died while he was still in another's mind? Would he simply become another cast member in the nightmares of Gavon Stills? Would he fade into nothingness? He really didn't know. One thing was certain though. The outcome of this was not going to be good for him.

The professor then shot him a devilish grin. "Let's find out." With that said Dr. Stills slammed the door and Jonathan closed his eyes. It didn't feel as bad as he thought it would. In fact it didn't feel like anything at all. For a second he thought that he must have been immediately transported to Heaven. But then he opened his eyes, the door was closed, which meant his body was dead, or at least dying, and he was still here. He wasn't at the gates of heaven or on his way to hell. It was as if nothing had happened. The young man looked at him and shrugged. "Well, well, what to do with you now?"

The monk did not speak. He was now the prisoner of the very man he had just tried to kill. Then there was a noise from behind him. The vines holding him turned him so he could see what, presumably, was his fate. In front of him were three doors made of what looked like rusty iron. "Pick one," his captor instructed as the vines released him.

Jonathan was fairly certain that none of these doors concealed anything that was going to be pleasant. They probably all led to the same place, Stills was just toying with him. But he turned to Gavon anyway and was going to ask what was behind the first door, but stopped dead.

Where the professor had been standing a few seconds before now stood the very embodiment of evil, Lucifer himself! It was as he'd been told. This man was evil! He was the prince of darkness. He had been sent to Hell. How was this possible? He'd always done the church's work.

The devil looked as he had always pictured him. Grey skin was pulled tight over a human skull with horns not unlike those of a ram sprouting from his forehead. Where there should have been eyes there were two small flames dancing mischievously in empty sockets. The demon was clad in black scale armor with ragged looking bat wings spreading behind him. In his clawed hand he held a smoking trident. Interestingly in the other he held a martini glass.

Jonathan was filled with terror and he stepped back. When he did, the door opened and he was falling. Finally the monk hit what he assumed was a stone floor. The pudgy man sat up and looked around, was he in Hell? There didn't appear to be any weeping, wailing, or gnashing of teeth as he'd been told about in Sunday school. In fact there was no sound at all, just a mime doing that stupid trapped in a box thing.

"No, you aren't in Hell," said a familiar voice from behind him. "And I'm not the devil."

He quickly turned and saw Gavon. The devil was gone, and for that he was glad, but he still was not happy to see this man. "At least not the Hell you are thinking of. For the time being you are my…guest. At least until I figure out what to do with you. But in the meantime enjoy the entertainment." He gestured to the mime, who was beginning to repeat his rather short routine. The professor grinned and said, "Oh yes, and I guess you will want some music as well."

From seemingly out of the air came the familiar sound of "Um Bop" by Hansen, and then his captor was gone. Jonathan couldn't help but wonder why such a song would be the listening choice for someone like Doctor Stills he'd expected something by Metallica or Korn. But after the fourth repetition of the song he realized why. He was trapped in a hell of Gavon's making.

"Damn you Stills!" was the last thing the young professor heard before emerging from his dream in a fit of hysterical laughter. That was certainly a worse fate than death, at least from his standpoint. He opened his eyes and was back in the real world. The faces of his companions were confused and concerned.

"What just happened?" Lynn asked warily.

Gavon just put up his hand to stop the inevitable onslaught of questions. "One down," was all he had to say. He would explain what had happened later. In truth he still needed time to figure it out.

On the other side of the door Arthur Tarvis stepped back in disgust as Jonathan's body slumped to the floor. He just lay there twitching as blood began to seep from his eyes, nose, ears, and mouth. Something had gone seriously wrong and now it was pretty certain that they were all going to die. The only question was how and when. The captain looked at the monk's now mostly still body. He wasn't very optimistic of their treatment once they were caught. But who could blame them, they had seen their friends and students ripped apart by the very creatures that Devaney had sent. If the positions were reversed, he wouldn't show any mercy either. But then again, mercy was something that was entirely beyond Arthur's comprehension.

The captain looked at his two remaining companions. He knew that the game was over. Tarvis could stay in here and cower until they broke down the door. Or he could go out and face them. The choice was pretty obvious for him. At least he would die on his feet, instead of hiding like a rat.

The mariner dropped to the floor and changed into what they had made him into. He was now ready. He stood up and reached for the door. The last thing he heard before a round from Lynn's pistol tore through his gray matter was Brother Samuel's voice, "What are you doing?!"

Chapter 49

Gavon's explanation would have to wait until later. The wheel on the door had begun to turn. It swung open, knocking Quintus to the side. Doctor Stills looked up at the face of yet another Diatritha coming through the door. The creature bore down on the professor, who was still kneeling on the floor. Ironically, even as the creature came closer, the professor somehow knew that this was not the end for him. Something inside the Texan had come alive after the encounter with Brother Jonathan, and he couldn't see the future exactly, but he knew that he would not be killed in the next few minutes.

He managed to get is hand up in between the creature and himself. But it wasn't a defensive gesture at all. To everyone's surprise he was actually giving the creature the finger.

If Brother Samuel's voice was the last thing that Arthur Tarvis heard, then Gavon's face blowing kisses behind his extended middle finger was the last thing he saw. The loud report of the .45 told Gavon the fate of his opponent as much as the gaping hole in the creature's head and the morbid Rorschach test the blood made on the wall.

The great hairy beast hit Doctor Stills hard, but his limp form didn't really do any damage. The professor managed to roll the heavy body off of him and join the others after picking up his own weapon. He found the ship's doctor and Brother Samuel cowering in the corner, while Lynn, Quintus, and Gerald pointed their weapons at them. They looked quite scared, except for one thing. Samuel's eyes didn't convey the same emotion as the rest of his body.

Gavon put his hand on Lynn's shoulder and was about to thank her, but she didn't react at all. The young woman seemed to be frozen. He didn't say a word, but leveled his weapon at the monk and squeezed the trigger. There was a loud crack as the rifle discharged and then confusion. The monk jerked a little as the bullet passed through his head, but then he slumped forward and didn't move. The doctor screamed and covered his head defensively, as if it would do any good. Doctor Levandusky began to fall to the floor, but was stopped by her lover's arms.

"What the hell did you do that for?" Quintus yelled. "He could have had information."

Gavon was about to answer, but Lynn spoke instead. "Thanks baby."

The adventurer looked at her questioningly and then nodded his head as he realized what had happened. Samuel had invaded her mind as Jonathan had done to Doctor Stills. By killing the monk's body he had created just the chance Lynn needed to take control. But she had been much kinder than her lover. The young woman had chosen to completely destroy the invader, rather than condemn him to the same kind of hell that now held Jonathan. Although she did send him into oblivion, the part of his consciousness that had given him his power was incorporated into her being. Her mind reached out and touched Gavon's and he knew that she was alright.

Quintus kicked the doctor, and not in a gentle fashion. "No, please don't kill me!" was all that he could say.

"Drop your hands and look at me, or I'll shoot you. But I might not be as kind as my friend here. You have a lot of parts you can survive without."

Amazingly, the doctor complied. Vale motioned for the students to leave the room. Once they had, the frightened man was very forthcoming with his knowledge. Of course some of the adventurer's techniques for extracting information from someone were not exactly approved by the Geneva Convention, but they were, none the less, effective.

The southerner began by slapping the frightened doctor in the face, and moved on from there. At first the prisoner refused to say anything. But after trying a few things Quintus smiled and asked Gavon to bring him a paper towel, a serving spoon, a paper clip, and three rubber-bands. Then he looked at the terrified man and grinned like an idiot. Doctor Stills looked slightly confused and shook his head a little before turning to leave. But before he could even get to the door the doctor was telling a now amused Quintus anything he wanted to know rather than find out what those particular items could be used for.

Devaney had planned to finish off Linus, Lisa, and Carl. Then he would travel to Rome for reassignment or as he hoped, retirement. After Quintus was satisfied that there was no more information to be had from the prisoner, he was bound with chains and ropes and placed in the still smoky cargo hold. Gavon was a little amused by the site of the terrified man hog tied with a dirty sock stuffed in his mouth as the students carried him away. The professor even smiled a little as the group dropped the doctor, then after a few steps, dropped him again.

Quintus Vale looked at the destroyed satellite phone and cursed out loud. The radio was in the same condition. There was no way to call anyone to help the others who were still in Anchorage with Devaney. This left little choice, they would have to make their best speed back and hope they would be in time. But it would take nearly two weeks with the sea being full of ice.

Gavon took the wheel as Quintus and Lynn began assessing whether there was any more damage that they could find. The ship was painfully slow, but since there was no choice they simply did what they could to pass the time. The three took turns staying on the bridge and watching the incapacitated Englishman. Gerald and Kumar took turns guarding the prisoner. And after a day or so, the other students began to help as well.

Chapter 50

Things calmed down as much as could be expected after the bodies were removed by Quintus and Doctor Stills, in an attempt to save the others any more emotional trauma. But it was clear that some of the students would never be the same. Logan was recovering nicely though, and not surprisingly the first thing he asked for when he regained consciousness was a beer. Needless to say he got it.

The students had begun to talk about what they would do once they got back to the real world. This prompted Gavon and Lynn to discuss the same thing. But, unlike the students, they realized that going back to their old lives was pretty unlikely.

One night after everyone else was asleep the two professors went to the bridge to talk to Quintus. They found him sitting with his feet propped up on the ship's control panel sipping from his flask. Oddly Logan was present as well, beer in hand, which wasn't odd at all. He was sitting in a chair with a blanket wrapped around him, and was wearing the same stupid hat that the captain had been wearing the first time the Englishman had met him. He still looked bad, but he was not quite as pale as he had been. They were on a straight heading for a while, so there was not much need for a lot of people keeping watch, at least not for the next few hours.

He looked up as they entered and nodded. "Are we interrupting anything?" Lynn asked in a joking manner.

"No, but you just missed the strippers and the midget jugglers," Logan coughed. His condition had done little to curb his sarcasm.

Lynn and Gavon laughed. "What are you doing here Logan? You should be in bed." Stills looked concerned for his friend.

"I actually needed to talk to Quintus about some things. But I assume that's why you're here as well."

Logan was right of course. So the pair sat down for what would probably be a long discussion. "So what do we do now?" Dr. Stills asked.

"I assume you mean after we get to Anchorage?" the adventurer asked.

"Of course," the young woman answered. "We aren't going to be able to go back to our lives are we?"

"I'm afraid not. It would be too dangerous for you and everyone you know." Vale looked out at the ocean. He'd had this discussion with so many people. But it was still difficult.

"I figured you'd say that." Doctor Stills sighed. "They will always be looking for us. Won't they?"

"Yes, they've done it before. No matter what happens in Anchorage, Gavon Stills, Lynn Levandusky, and Logan Fry died in the wilds of Alaska. You'll have to start new lives, become new people. Would you mind being Australians?"

"How are we going to do that?" Lynn looked skeptical.

"We have people who help people do just that. They can set you up in a new place, with a new identity. Think of them as a global witness protection program. We even have plastic surgeons for extreme situations. But I don't think that it will be necessary in your case."

"Does it really work?" Lynn asked.

"Most of the time, yes. We've only had a few cases where the people we were hiding were discovered. And those cases were the result of the people involved doing something that we specifically said that they shouldn't, in other words, something stupid. But there is another option."

"What would that be?" Logan asked.

"You could join us." Quintus said evenly.

"You mean like you, traveling all over the world looking for things that go bump in the night?" Gavon asked.

Quintus looked back and smiled. "Yep, just like me. You three would make good additions. We only extend this offer to the most exceptional people, and that certainly includes you three. Besides, what else do you have to do?"

"What about the students?" Lynn asked.

"Gerald might hold some promise, but I don't think that this life would suit the others. They will have to be given new identities. They did well considering the situation. But I don't think that any of them are cut out for this sort of thing. Anyway for a number of reasons they can't go back to the world they knew."

"Why not? If they choose to take that risk, it's their choice." Gavon sounded annoyed.

"The most obvious answer is that they will be dead in a week. The church can't and won't let this information become public. But they would also endanger everyone they had contact with. We can't let more people get drawn in to this thing than we have to."

Gavon started to say something, but then decided against it. He reached up, grabbed his hair with both hands, and sighed. Quintus was right. There really was no way to go back. He and Lynn had a hard decision to make. As for Logan, he had already decided.

"Count me in." The Brit coughed. I really think that this is worth doing, especially after all we've seen. Not to mention with what I know. I could be very useful to you. Besides, I still would like to get some more revenge. What say you Gav? Lynn?"

The lovers looked at each other. Then Stills turned to Quintus and

Logan. "We have to think about this. We'll let you know in Anchorage."

The pair then took their leave of the adventurer and the Englishman. The walk back to their room was a long and silent one. Each was lost in thought, although these thoughts were of the same things.

Once the pair was back in the privacy of their room, Gavon looked at Lynn. "Well, I know what my vote is."

"Me too", she said as she looked back at the man she had grown more and more in love with. There was really no discussion. Both agreed that there really was only one reasonable option. So they decided to tell Quintus about it once they were in Anchorage.

Chapter 51

The Perseverance docked in the Anchorage harbor a few days later. Three people left the ship and immediately went to the hospital. Finally after a couple of hours of bureaucratic bullshit, Lynn and Gavon were able to talk to a doctor.

They knew immediately what he was going to say. The look on his face told them everything. "I'm sorry," he said. "He didn't make it."

"Carl?" Doctor Stills looked at the floor and sighed. He had figured that the student would probably not survive.

"You don't know do you?" The young doctor sat down and began to tell them what had happened.

Carl had come out of his coma and had begun to recover. And of course Lisa had never left his side. Devaney had gone to visit the sick man every day, and to the hospital staff this seemed reasonable since his condition seemed to get worse by the day.

Then one day there was a loud noise in the patient's room and the priest landed on his back outside the door with a startled look on his face. To everyone's surprise standing in the doorway was Lisa, all 100 pounds of her, and she looked like she was ready to kill someone.

Before anyone could say anything, the woman spoke. "Keep this...person away from us."

An orderly and two nurses looked down at the man on the floor who was now glaring back at Lisa. Finally the hospital security showed up and despite Marco's attempts to convince them that he should be allowed to stay, the two security guards escorted him to the door and told him not to come back. The angry priest stood there for a moment and then stormed off into the darkness.

Lisa had become pretty good friends with the entire hospital staff, which was not surprising since she was essentially living there while Carl was ill. So it was not surprising that they took her side without question.

The very next day, the young man had begun to recover. And after a week, he opened his eyes for the first time since the night he had fallen ill. Lisa had been so excited by his recovery that she had hardly given any thought to the fact that Linus had begun to visit them less and less often. He had said that he simply didn't feel well. And finally the director stopped showing up at all.

One day while the two students were eating breakfast, one of the nurses entered the room. Her name was Jenny, and in spite of her usual cheerful demeanor, today she was not laughing. In fact she looked like someone who was about to deliver a terrible message, and in fact she was.

As soon as the two looked up, they realized that something had happened.

"What is it?" Carl asked.

"It's your friend Director Mitchell," She said slowly.

"What's wrong? Has he come down with whatever I had now?"

"No…He's dead."

"WHAT!?" The pair shouted in unison.

"The police found him this morning in an alleyway. They said it looked like he had been there at least a day."

Lisa looked puzzled, even though she knew what had happened. "Do they know who killed him?" She managed as the tears began to develop.

"They don't think he was murdered. They think he died of exposure."

"They are wrong!" Lisa shouted. Mitchell may have been one of the most boring and irritating men in the world, but he was definitely smart enough to avoid dying from the cold when he was only a block or so from his hotel. Lisa knew that it must be the priest.

Shortly after that the two students had left the hospital and gotten on a plane bound for the lower 48 states. But no one knew exactly where they were headed.

The doctor looked at Lynn, "She asked me to give you this." He then handed Lynn a small envelope.

The young woman looked at Gavon and then quickly opened it. Inside was a small piece of stone. It looked like granite, but had small blue crystals in it. Lynn looked at the piece for a moment and smiled a little bit. "I know where they're going."

The knowledge that the two students were alive, or at least they had been a week ago brought some comfort, but the two professors were still filled with grief at the news of the death of yet another friend. It seemed to hit them both at the same moment and Lynn leaned her head onto Gavon's shoulder in an attempt to muffle her already silent sobs. Linus had been a pain in the ass, but both of them had at least on some level thought of him as a friend.

"What about the priest?" Doctor Stills asked, summoning all his will power to keep the tears from coming.

"I don't know. I haven't seen him in some time. He said that he would contact the ship and give them the news. I guess you never got the message. Once again I'm sorry for your loss." The doctor then stood up and with one last look at the pair walked away to deal with his other patients.

After a few moments the two professors were able to compose themselves a little. Finally Lynn looked up at Quintus who was, as always, moving his eyes around the immediate area in a constant search for anything that might be remotely dangerous. When she was sure that no one was in ear shot she simply said, "They're in Llano Texas."

The adventurer looked at her and nodded. Most people would have asked her how she knew, but Quintus, like Stills, had gotten used to Lynn being right. Then he went over to a nearby pay phone and began dialing. A short time later he returned. "Some of our people are on the way to Llano to keep an eye on Carl and Lisa. I told them to just protect them, and not make any kind of contact. That is something someone they trust will have to do. Otherwise they will probably run again."

"I guess that means us doesn't it?" Gavon looked at Lynn, who nodded in agreement. "What about us, and the rest of the survivors?"

"People are on the way. They should be here by tomorrow. After that we will all be new people with new identities. I may extend my offer to Carl and Lisa as well. If they were resourceful enough to escape from someone like Devaney then they certainly have what it takes to join us. But like you two, it will be their decision."

"So this is it, the end. Right?" Lynn asked.

"Yes, I guess it is. There are still a few details to work out, but I think that for the most part your involvement in this is over, if that is what you choose. By the way what did you two decide?"

The young woman looked at her lover and he nodded. Then the pair gave Quintus their answer. He looked back at them with a slightly confused look on his face. Part of him was happy for them, and part of them wanted to try to make them reconsider. He started to open his mouth when Lynn spoke, "It's our decision."

The adventurer looked at the pair and nodded. "How did you know where they are anyway?"

Lynn smiled "That rock is called Llanite. It is only found in one place...Llano."

Quintus Vale nodded and smiled a little. Gavon definitely had quite a woman.

The group walked back to the docks. Once they were back on the ship, the southerner began to tell everyone what was going to happen to them now. Bell Ringers like Quintus were on the way to help relocate everyone and help with the transition process. Doctor Stills looked at his love and kissed her on the forehead. Their horrific ordeal was over. It hadn't ended like he'd hoped, but at least they were both still breathing. It was time to begin their new life, together.

Chapter 52

The old man emerged from his house and looked around. It was a beautiful spring morning in Crete. He loved this time of the day, especially in the Mediterranean. The smell of the bread cooking, the sounds of the birds chirping, all made him feel at ease. This was a wonderful place to start over.

The people in this small village looked up to him and listened to what he had to stay. It was nice to feel important again. In his early days as a priest right out of seminary he had felt like this. The old man took a deep breath and began to recite his usual morning prayer as the wind rustled his silver hair ever so slightly. "This is the day that the lord hath made, rejoice and be glad in it." He paused for a moment. There were usually people walking the streets when he started his day. But the priest had begun a little earlier today. There was still much to do. Many of these people had strayed away from the lord and needed to be brought back into the fold.

The old priest turned to close his door after he finished praying and then collapsed to the ground. He had never seen the gunman, or heard the shot. How could he have? The man who had fired was nearly half a mile away. Marco Devaney, powerful as he was, now lay dead in the street with bits of brain and skull plastering his door. A fitting testament to the lives he had helped to destroy.

People began to run over to see what had happened. Someone yelled for a doctor, but everyone knew that it was too late. The hole in his head was big enough to fit a medium sized coin. The place where the bullet had exited, the man's face, was now little more than a red mass of gore and bone fragments. Whoever had done this had used a large enough bullet to put down an elephant, insuring that there would be no recovery.

On a ridge outside of town two men began to casually walk down towards the beach and a waiting yacht. One was carrying a rifle. The other had a pair of binoculars around his neck. The one with the binoculars was in the process of dusting off his cowboy hat when he turned to the other and said, "Public school system my ass."

The other turned and smiled, then shrugged. He looked at the yacht anchored just off the beach. His sharp eyes could make out the shape of his wife, looking beautiful as always, standing on the deck in a bikini, her blonde hair blowing in the wind. The two waded out into the warm water and made it to the vessel.

"Well, I guess we'd better get out of here before anyone figures out what just happened," the man with the rifle said as he climbed the ladder of the ship and kissed his wife.

"How about Spain?" another voice came from the cabin of the ship. The man's voice betrayed the slightest hint of a British accent.

"I've always wanted to see Spain," a shorter younger woman with curly blonde hair answered as she leaned her head against another man in his early twenties.

"Sounds good to me. Do you need another beer…captain?"

"No I'm good," laughed the other.

"Some people never change," he thought. He held his wife as close as he could and said, "Now it's over."

The pair stood on the deck for a long while watching the Island of Crete slowly getting smaller. He kissed her and the two sat down to relax for the first time in months. Their new lives had officially begun.